A MAIL ORDER BRIDE FOR THE RANCHER

WESTERN BRIDES

BLYTHE CARVER

1

———

Jeremiah Connelly was up early that morning in May. His heart was heavy with sorrow, but he had to press on as if everything was normal. He was concerned that if he showed how much pain he was in, his mother and the women around him would shower him with attention and affection.

He gently recoiled at the thought. As much as he loved the ladies who helped his mother bring him up, he wasn't very keen on their hugs, kisses, and pinching of his cheeks. He was standing at that moment on the porch of the ranch that was now his. His with the passing of his father, a strong and bold man who had raised Jeremiah to be the man that he was, a man he could be proud of. A man they could both be proud of.

His father, Alexander Marian Connelly, had been a pillar of the community. Their small town of Low Branch, Texas, was going to sorely miss the beacon of light Alex Connelly had been. Jeremiah could only hope to mean half as much to the townsfolk as his father had.

As one of the founders of the town when he was just a young man and several years before Jeremiah was born, Alex had gone on to be a beloved mayor until he was stricken with tuberculosis. It took him in just under three years. He had suffered greatly in the meantime, and his position as mayor was taken over by his second, a good-hearted man named Nicholas Nickerson. Now he was the beloved mayor, and Jeremiah was gratified his father was succeeded by someone with the same brilliance, strength, and kindness.

Jeremiah took in a deep breath, holding back his emotions. He'd cried for his father the night of the man's death two weeks ago. Since then, if he shed a tear, it was behind closed doors. Never in front of his mother or the other women. He had to be strong. He had to be like his father.

There were several buggies gathered in front of

the ranch in the large dirt lot that made a circle around a lawn of green accessorized by patches of various types and colors of flowers and a statue in the middle of a leaping horse.

Jeremiah's uncle had sculpted that horse with his own hands. He'd presented it to Alex the day the ranch was purchased, and Alex became a wealthy man.

"Jeremiah?"

He turned to see his mother approaching from behind him. She looked elegant in her dark green gown. She wore a thin black veil over her face to represent mourning.

"How are you, darling?" she asked, taking his arm and squeezing it. "You do look distraught."

"I'm not... I mean, I *am* distraught, of course, Mother, I'm just... I'm just thinking, that's all. Thinking about what my responsibilities around here are now that Pa is gone."

"Oh, you know it won't change much," his mother replied in her typical stern but gentle way of speaking. "You've been the man around here since your father was struck with illness. You already do almost everything as it is."

Jeremiah knew his mother was only half-right. He had, indeed, been doing a great deal of the work around the ranch. A lot of the hands-on work that he'd already been doing, plus picking up the slack where his father was no longer able to help out.

But now, he would have everything else that his father did and was capable of doing even while he was sick. He made a lot of decisions, as his mind was clear for much of the time until the very end when the pain was too much, and he was put on medications that made him sleep most of the time.

Now everything would be left up to Jeremiah. It was up to him to sign the checks and order supplies and make decisions for every part of the ranch and its business.

"Come on inside," his mother urged him. "Benjamin wants to read the will. I think he wants to go home to his family. His little girl is having a birthday today."

Jeremiah tried not to feel any resentment that his lawyer and friend wanted to hurry through his father's will so he could get home. It was a petty reaction, he decided.

So he buried it with the rest of his pain.

They had barely slipped into their seats before Benjamin Ratcliffe, their family lawyer, was reading from the will. When he got past all the legal wording at the beginning, he slowed down and began flipping his eyes up to look at Jeremiah. "All right, now... this is the part you've been waiting for. It has to do with leaving his possessions. I won't make you wait any longer."

Jeremiah sat and listened, as hard and cold as a stone, stunned into absolute silence by what the lawyer proceeded to say, growing more and more anxious as time went on.

"After the bequeathed amounts mentioned at the end of this section, anything remaining will be given to my son, my only heir, Jeremiah, with the stipulation that he is married within three months of the reading of this will."

Jeremiah stiffened, cold chills sliding up his arms and down his spine. His eyes snapped to Benjamin, narrowing angrily.

"What was that? What was that about marriage?"

Benjamin stopped, his face turning bright red. He swallowed hard and blinked at Jeremiah. "That's what it says, Jeremiah."

"Well, can I get around that?" Jeremiah demanded, crossing his arms over his chest. "I'm not even courting anyone. I have no sweetheart to speak of. I work too much to think about courting a woman. I would want to give her my full time. I don't..." He stopped, letting his words trail off. By the look on Benjamin's face, he could tell he was wasting his breath.

He shook his head, flabbergasted at the right hook surprise his beloved father had left him.

"Well, what happens if I don't get married within three months?" he asked, trying not to get upset. There had to be a way out of this.

"The ranch and the entire estate will go to your uncle."

All eyes turned to Jeremiah's uncle, Daniel Connelly, who was as successful and wealthy due to his own efforts and hard work. Daniel's thick grey eyebrows shot up, as did his hands, his palms out.

"I didn't know," he said quickly. "Alex knew I had my eye on the land and ideas for ways to make it better, but I didn't know about this."

Jeremiah sighed. "I don't believe this."

"Good luck, though," Daniel added. "I mean that."

2

———

"Did you know about this, Mother?" Jeremiah tried to keep his tone even. He was not about to disrespect his mother. Aggravation was surging in him, though, making it difficult to keep calm.

Everyone had gone. On his way out, Jeremiah's uncle had shaken Jeremiah's hand and told him there would be no pressure from his end.

"I'll give you a couple extra few days if you need it," he'd said.

And that was it.

The man had hopped down the stairs and gone to his buggy, talking to the foreman of his ranch, who went with him everywhere like a bodyguard.

Jeremiah was under the impression the two men had been friends since they were boys, and Daniel relied on the man to help him make good business decisions.

"I didn't know anything about it," Clarice replied, shaking her head. She was bundled up in a shawl as the May day had turned a bit windy and chilly. They were on the porch once more, as Jeremiah had begun to feel stuffy inside the house.

"Do you think Uncle Daniel knew? He seemed pretty confident when he said he'd give me a couple of days."

"I don't know if he knew, Jeremiah," his mother answered, sighing heavily. She was an overly dramatic woman as it was. Jeremiah tried to keep his personal business away from her because of that. She might try fainting, which would require him to give her more attention than he had time for. Besides, it was he who had been done wrong.

"Why else would he bring Albert with him?" Jeremiah stormed. He took to his feet, bounding up and down the porch in front of his mother. A squeaking floorboard got his attention. Repairs on the porch were the last thing he needed.

Frustrated almost to the breaking point, Jeremiah stopped at the pole of the railing and slapped one hand flat against it. It stung his palm, but he didn't care.

"I don't even have a woman on my arm," he raged, glaring out over the land he thought was now his. "Why would he want me to suddenly grab a woman and share all of this with her? Who deserves that? How could I possibly find a woman worthy of living here, becoming a member of our family in just three months? Did he somehow think I had a sweetheart?"

His mother didn't answer. He looked over his shoulder at her. She was looking down at her hands, which she'd bundled in the ends of the long shawl she was wearing over her shoulders and head. He stared at her, wondering just how much she knew.

Could his mother be lying to him? If she was, exactly what was she lying about? How much had she truly known about this scheme of his father's?

"Mother?" He knew his voice was menacing, but he couldn't help it. She was pushing the limit with him. "What did you do?"

"I didn't tell him you had a sweetheart, Jeremiah." His mother let out a sharp breath as she spoke and flapped the ends of her shawl nervously. She lifted her eyes but not to look at him. She stared away from him at the trees on the other side of the lawn. When she moved her eyes, it was only as far as the statue.

"Mother," Jeremiah barked. "What did you do?"

"Well, he was upset," Clarice exclaimed, squeezing her hands together, her voice as tight as her jaw. "He needed some reassurance that there would be an heir. He was just as concerned about it as I was, you know."

Jeremiah pulled in a sharp breath. "But, Mother." He crossed over to her chair and got down on one knee, looking at her with pleading eyes. "You know I am not interested in finding a woman until I can give her the time she deserves. I want to give my love every minute I can and make her happy so she knows how important she is. I can't do that if I'm always working. Right now is the worst time for me to start something with a woman since I will have all of Pa's additional work he was still doing on *me* every day. I have to learn a schedule and get used to it before I can devote time to a woman."

His mother didn't say anything at first. She wouldn't look at him either.

When she finally did, he saw she had tears in her eyes.

"I... I didn't realize he would try to force this, Jeremiah. I really didn't tell him you had a sweetheart. I just told him a week before he passed that there seemed to be something going on between you and Betty at the market."

Tingles covered Jeremiah's body. His voice was quiet when he said, "Betty Copperfield?"

She looked away from him again, blinking quickly. She knew what she'd done was wrong.

"I didn't know he was going to force it. To push you. I didn't mean anything when I said it. I was only trying to cheer him up."

Jeremiah thought for a moment about Betty Copperfield. He tried to recall any time she had flirted with him or given him the impression she wanted to spend time with him. He couldn't recall any such time. Plus, he was fairly certain she was at least ten years older than him. He didn't mind the thought of being with an older woman. But the connection it would take for them to become a couple wasn't there. If it was, it would have already manifested itself. He'd gone in the supply shop plenty of times.

His heart hurt when he looked at his mother. Tears rolled down her cheeks. She still couldn't look at him.

His anger dissipated as quickly as it had come over him. He pulled in a deep breath and held it for a moment, pushing up to his feet with one hand on the edge of the porch table next to his mother and the other one on the armrest of her chair.

He looked down at her, hesitating before lowering himself to give her a hug.

"I'm sorry, Mother. I didn't mean to upset you. I know you miss Pa so much. I know you do. I do, too."

"I only… wanted him to… be happier…" his mother gulped out between sobs. "If… if you could have seen him smile. Son, it made him so happy to think you might have found love. I swear to you, I didn't know he would push it like this. I didn't know he would do this to you."

"It's all right, Mother. It's all right."

He hugged her some more, patting her on the back. He would find a way out of this or find a way to deal with it. One way or another, the ranch would be his.

As he rose back up to his feet, his eyes settled on an open magazine on the table beside him. His vision focused on an ad. The title was Find a Bride/Become a Bride.

He couldn't believe it. It had to be a sign from

God. He snatched up the paper and, giving his mother a final look of remorse, sauntered inside, hoping she wouldn't ask him what he was doing with her magazine.

3

"Such a dreary day." Isabelle Lawton rolled her eyes and turned away from the window. She enjoyed the battering of the water against the glass, but that was about the only thing she liked about a rainy day in Berkenshire, Va. It was cold, gray, and *dreary*. It made her want to sleep all day, and that wasn't like her. She prided herself on being energetic and always ready to do something fun and adventurous.

She'd already decided to go into town and see her friend, Margie. She didn't like to make plans and not keep them. So she dressed accordingly and was pleased when she stepped out to see the morning rain had dissipated and the sun was showing its bright, warm face, drying up the mud puddles.

She longed to get out and explore the world. So far, she wasn't having any luck at that. In all of her twenty-one years, she'd never been past the town limits of Berkenshire. She was itching for it, though.

Isabelle hadn't been raised with a great deal of wealth. The little cottage she lived in was well-maintained by her aunt and uncle, who were dear to her but had lives of their own.

Delilah and Walter Banks had taken care of her since her parents died in the fire that consumed their house. Delilah, called Lila, was Isabelle's mother's sister. She taught Isabelle everything she needed to know to be out on her own, and the Banks promptly left town to do some traveling of their own. They gave Isabelle the cottage, saying that if they ever returned, they expected her to have abandoned it for adventures of her own, or they would all be living together there.

She thought about them all the time. She wouldn't have minded if they'd wanted to come back and stay. She often got lonely.

It was difficult for someone like her to live alone. She wasn't in need of money because her aunt and uncle sent her a monthly allowance and had since they'd left when she was sixteen. She'd learned to survive quite well on the allowance, even keeping some back in case she needed a savings of some sort.

It wasn't much, but it was enough for a train ticket somewhere. She always thought the longer she saved, the further away she'd be able to get.

But time had passed, and she'd settled into a nice routine. She got up at the same time every day and went to sleep that night on time, too. Isabelle didn't have an exciting life, but that didn't mean she never would.

Isabelle slowed down the horse pulling her buggy through Berkenshire main street. Tugging on the left rein, she pulled the buggy over and climbed down. As she walked around the buggy, she brushed her hands down her skirt to smooth it out.

"Well, hello there."

Her heart plummeted into her stomach when she heard a voice she'd been hoping she wouldn't hear. How did she not see him before she pulled over? He had to have been hiding from her or walking just behind her buggy until she pulled over. She came to the conclusion it was the latter.

She struggled not to let her face reveal what she was thinking.

"Hello, Percy," she said through pinched lips.

The mayor was a good man. How he'd spawned

Percy, who was not a gentleman of any sort, was a mystery.

Percy sauntered over as if he was the smoothest man on the planet. The look on his face reflected that thought, as well.

"How are you doing, dear? You look lovely."

Percy's compliments did nothing for Isabelle. He was a decent-looking man. Some women might even call him handsome. He had dark brown hair that swept and waved over his head like small dark ocean waves. His eyes were a piercing brown, narrow with naturally shaded eyelids. His face was sculpted and shaped so his features fit quite well together.

But the handsome exterior didn't hide the slimy interior Isabelle was aware of. His agenda to have Isabelle as his wife was well-known. But her disdain was just as widely known. It seemed like Percy was the only one who didn't know that. Or he just wouldn't accept that Isabelle wasn't interested in him that way.

In reality, she wasn't interested in him in any way. She didn't want to be friends with him. She certainly didn't want anything *more* than that. And if she had her way, she'd be leaving town on the first train out of Virginia.

"Have dinner with me, my dear," Percy said,

holding out his hand as if she wanted to touch him at all. She glanced down at it, suddenly nervous because she was about to reject it, and that might make him angry. It wasn't a good idea to upset the mayor's son—even if chances were good no action would be taken as a result.

Mayor Barney Andrews was a good enough man—a decent fellow who seemed to want to do right by the sleepy riverside town. When it came to his son, however, he had a blind spot. He was weak where Percy was concerned, having a deep love for the boy despite his obvious flaws.

"I... I—"

"Oh, Isabelle..." Now her name was called in a sing-song way that lifted her heart up instead of bringing it down. She stepped to the side and smiled wide at Margie Milkins, who had apparently just stepped out of her dress shop when Isabelle pulled the buggy over. She'd been intending to go to Margie's shop and was pleased her friend had seen what was going on. She was truly a guardian angel.

Isabelle stretched both arms toward her friend, taking long steps directly past Percy to the woman. Margie did the same, and the two women grasped hands. They leaned toward each other, giving "air kisses" on either side of their faces.

"Oh, you do look lovely, yes. Oh, doesn't she look —" Margie turned to Percy. Isabelle looked on with amusement as Margie wrinkled her forehead and stared the man up and down. "Oh, it's you. How are you, Percy? Need some supplies from my shop?"

Percy narrowed his eyes at the woman. Isabelle was fully aware the two didn't get along. Then again, Percy didn't get along well with anyone.

"Not right now, thank you. And you are interrupting our conversation. I had just asked the dear lady to join me for dinner."

"Well, she can't," Margie said bluntly, her face not registering any emotion at all. "She has plans."

Percy's eyes narrowed even more, reminding Isabelle of a snake.

"Is that so?" He turned to Isabelle. "What plans do you have?"

"She's coming over to my h—"

Both Margie's and Isabelle's eyes opened wide when Percy held up one hand directly in front of Margie's face as if to shut her up completely and block her out.

"I asked Isabelle the question, Margie," he said in a cold voice.

Margie's eyebrows shot up, and she gasped loudly.

"Percy," Isabelle exclaimed. "How rude of you."

Percy looked completely innocent. He gave her a nonchalant glance before tilting his head to the side. "I simply want you to tell me what plans you have this evening without being influenced by your little friend here."

Isabelle wondered what about his behavior made Percy think she would ever consider courting him. It would not be a match made in Heaven, she was sure of that.

Isabelle gave him a cold look, unhappy by his treatment of her good friend like a nonhuman.

"I am going to her house for dinner and a few games of cards," she supplied the excuse. She hated to lie, but sometimes it was necessary. She stomped past him, tilting her head up and jutting out her chin. "Thank you, Percy," she said as she went by. "Maybe another time."

"There's never another time," Percy yelled.

For a moment, she was afraid he was going to come into the dress shop after her. But Margie turned the lock inside.

"You're fine now, Isabelle," Margie murmured while gathering her friend in her arms. You're going to be fine now. I promise."

4

____

Isabelle was able to glance back in time to see what reaction Percy had to Margie's interference. The look on his face was priceless. She felt a giggle rise up in her chest, and then guilt immediately followed. She couldn't help not wanting to be around Percy any more than she had to be.

He was loathsome.

He spun around and stomped off, much to her relief.

Isabelle turned back with a sigh, shaking her head at her friend. "I don't know what to do anymore, Margie. I feel so, I don't know, so closed. It's like I never go anywhere or do anything interesting."

Margie's eyebrows lifted. "But you don't do anything or go anywhere interesting. Where would you go? What would you do? Berkenshire isn't the most exciting place in the world. I doubt it registers as more than a dot on the map. Come over here, dear. Sit down and talk to me."

The woman held out one hand. Isabelle was overcome with affection for her friend.

"I guess I can spare a few minutes to sit down," she said sarcastically. "I don't have anything better to do."

Margie pretended to be offended by the remark, but it was easy to see she was only joking when she said, "Well, that doesn't make me feel all that wonderful."

Isabelle had to giggle, taking a chair by the wood stove near the back of the small store. It was sometimes occupied by Margie's old papa, her grandfather, who was old when he had Margie's father and seemed ancient to both the young ladies now.

"Where's Gramps?" Isabelle asked, peering toward the back of the store down a narrow hallway. There were rooms down that way, but Isabelle didn't know what they were used for.

"He's taking a nap," Margie replied, pulling a chair closer to Isabelle and dropping down in it. She leaned forward, grabbing Isabelle's hands in hers. "You have to make a plan, Isabelle. You aren't going to get away from Percy."

"I know," Isabelle replied in a resigned voice. "I don't know what to do. I'm really... really quite lost."

An overwhelming sadness pulled Isabelle's shoulders down. Only the squeezing of her hands by Margie brought her out of her depressed state.

"Now, now," the woman said vehemently. "Don't you think like that. You aren't to blame for being attractive and charming and brilliant and beautiful."

"Oh my goodness." Isabelle blushed to the roots of her hair, rolling her eyes and smiling. "You are too flattering. I'm embarrassed."

Margie just laughed. "Don't be silly, my girl. You deserve to be praised like that every day. By someone you want to praise you. Not that ol' Percy. He's such a dirty dog."

"I know." Isabelle shivered a little, and her own reaction made her chuckle. "So, what do you suggest I do about it?"

She lifted her gaze to her friend's face and was just in time to see an idea obviously come to Margie, whose eyes opened wide. She seemed to rise up from the chair, her eyes elsewhere. Isabelle watched and turned in the chair as Margie went over to the counter where the register sat and grabbed one of the magazines from the rack.

She flipped through it as she came back, lowering into the chair and leaning toward Isabelle.

"Look, I saw something in... in this one, I'm sure of it."

She looked up triumphantly, turning the newspaper around and shoving it in Isabelle's face. "What... what are you..." Isabelle pulled away, but Margie was excited, tapping the bottom half of the page she was showing Isabelle. Laughing, she also pulled away so Isabelle wouldn't lose her balance.

"I'm sorry, honey. I almost made you fall over. I was too excited. I just think this might be the very best thing for you right here. You can find a husband in one of these ads."

Isabelle widened her eyes, dropping them to the paper, which was now just about the right distance from her. She did see a list of ads and took the magazine from Margie.

"What is this?" she asked softly.

"Men out in the west are looking for women to come and marry them and give them families. I'm sure that would be something of an adventure, wouldn't it be?"

Isabelle had to admit that Margie was right. It

sounded bizarre, the strangest idea she'd ever heard. Travel to a completely different state in the middle of the country to marry a man she's never met? How did something like that work?

Isabelle was very interested in the prospect of going somewhere no one knew who she was or anything about her. She ran her eyes down the page, taking in the two rows of ads. In all, there were five in each row. Ten ads from men looking for a woman to marry. It was a little bit unbelievable, but it was certainly welcome in Isabelle's mind.

"It's... it's a new beginning," she murmured. "I can't believe there's even something like this available. Let's see. This one is a rancher in Wyoming. A widower. Three children. Hmmm." She continued looking, Margie hovering over her shoulder.

"What about that one?" Margie murmured, reaching around Isabelle and pointing at one near the bottom. "He's not a widower. And no children. Just starting out, it looks like. He sounds nice."

Isabelle read through the short ad several times before nodding. "I think this... Jeremiah Connelly sounds promising." She smiled at Margie. "Thanks for showing me this. I would never have known about it at all."

"Oh, you're welcome, my dear. Now, do you have

the supplies to write back? You have paper and a pen and ink and everything?"

Isabelle laughed softly. "You think of everything, don't you?"

Margie chuckled with her, standing straight once more. "Over here." She waved with one hand, and Isabelle got to her feet to follow her to a small desk the store used to display the items they had for sale that would be used in a desk. Ink, pen, paper, clips, everything one might need to keep good records.

"Here are two pieces of paper and a pen for two cents. And you can have an envelope for free, just because I know what you're doing with it."

"You're a true friend, Margie. Really." She smiled at the woman as she fished for the two pennies in her small coin purse.

All the way home, she thought about what she would say. Could she just describe herself as she was? An independent woman looking to get out and enjoy her life? That she wanted to make something of herself, and she felt like she was in a rut there in Berkenshire?

She didn't want to sound too negative.

By the time she reached her cottage, she knew what she wanted to say. She was anxious to get it on paper and send it off. It wasn't until she was walking in the front door that she thought she should have stayed in town, written the letter, and dropped it off with the Postmaster.

Giggling at her own ineptitude, she decided it would be nice to go back to town anyway. Maybe she would have dinner there. There wasn't anything else to do with her time.

DEAR MR. JEREMIAH CONNELLY, she wrote.

I have had the pleasure of reading your ad and would like to inquire if you are still looking for a woman to come from the east to be your wife. I am very interested in doing this. I want to leave my hometown of Berkenshire, Virginia, where I was born and raised by my Aunt and Uncle. I have no other relatives to speak of and feel very lonely quite often. I want to start a new life, and your offer sounds like something I would enjoy. Please write back when you can.

Yours sincerely,

Isabelle Lawton

5

Isabelle sat back in her chair. If things worked out the way she wanted, she wouldn't be in the cottage for much longer. She and Jeremiah Connelly had been corresponding by mail for six weeks. His last letter had intrigued her. He sounded like a generous, kind, attractive kind of man. They already knew they had a bond, as they enjoyed singing. It was something she'd had to drag out of him, and the slow way he responded to her inquiry in all three letters that followed the initial one was endearing to her.

When he finally admitted that he did have a good singing voice, he'd said he never believed it because his mother had praised him so highly. It just didn't seem like something his own mother praised him for was really a quality he had. It was his mother, after all.

But others had told him so, he said, so he guessed it must be true.

Isabelle was looking forward to singing with him. It would be so much fun. He said he had a friend who played the fiddle and another who played violin.

The whole prospect of going to Texas to be with Jeremiah Connelly was becoming more and more exciting as the days went by. She was now waiting anxiously for his next letter, hoping he was sending her a train ticket and an invitation. She knew that was where it was heading as his last letter asked if she was ready to move across the country. She'd said yes in her own most recent correspondence.

Isabelle closed her eyes and leaned her head back on the chair. She concentrated on the quiet, picking out the different sounds she could hear outside through the crack of her open window. A cool May breeze blew through, cooling her heated skin. She liked it warm, and the fireplace in front of her was blazing high, the flames licking the bricks of the chimney.

She could hear crickets outside, singing their sometimes annoying song. The sounds of the night creatures comforted Isabelle. Soon she would sit back and enjoy the music of Texas nights.

The crack of a stick outside being stepped on made her eyes snap open. She sat up abruptly. That was not an animal. She could tell because the moment the tree limb broke, all the sounds stopped. That was a conscious decision to stop moving. Animals didn't stop when they made noise. They stopped when something or a human around them made a noise.

Humans stopped when they alerted any listening ears to their presence when they didn't want to be heard.

Isabelle leaped to her feet and crossed the few feet to the fireplace. Her uncle's rifle rested patiently on the two hooks above the mantle. She snatched it off and yanked it open to stare down into the chamber. Two rounds were lodged there, waiting to be used.

She slammed the rifle closed and headed to the door. She yanked it open and was about to step out onto the porch to yell at the intruder.

She didn't have to threaten anyone. She nearly ran into Percy Andrews, who was holding a big bouquet of flowers.

"Good evening, Isabelle," he said, sweeping one

arm under him as he bowed to her. She instantly curled her lip and had to recover from her revulsion. She stayed where she was, setting the rifle behind the doorjamb, leaning it against the interior wall.

"Hello, Percy. What are you doing here? It's late."

He lifted his hand and slipped the small pocket watch from his vest pocket, looking at it skeptically. "It's only a quarter to nine. You don't look like you were ready for bed. I was passing by and thought I would stop and see how you are tonight."

She eyed the flowers in his hand. "Passing by with a bouquet of flowers?" she queried. "You do that often? Just walk around with a bunch of flowers in your hands? Or are they for your mother?"

Percy looked annoyed. He shoved the bouquet toward her. "No, they are for you. And I was just passing and stopped to buy them to bring to you. I don't know how many ways I can show you how I feel about you, Isabelle. You're a beautiful woman. My kind of woman. You're the woman for me. You always have been."

"So you've said," Isabelle replied, taking the flowers from him. "Thank you. They are lovely flowers. And I do know how you feel about me. Yes. You've told me. Over and over."

She moved to close the door, but he put his foot forward and blocked it from closing.

"Aren't you being a bit rude, Isabelle? I just gave you flowers. You should invite me in. We should talk."

Isabelle fought her instincts. She was angry at him and scared of him at the same time. She didn't want to feel any of those emotions.

"Percy, I wasn't in the mood for visitors tonight."

He looked incredibly downtrodden. As much as she wasn't attracted to him, she found it hard to be rude to him. He wasn't evil and would probably have been a good husband to her if she loved him.

But she had no feelings for him. The only thing she felt was sorry for him.

"Please let me in just for a little while. So we can talk. If you just let yourself get to know me, I know you'd see me the way I see you. We are meant to be, Isabelle. We are. I know it. I can feel it in here." He tapped his chest over his heart with pinched fingers. "Please. Let me have some time with you."

Isabelle's chest tightened with anxiety. "Percy... there can't be anything between us. I am leaving town soon. I am not interested in courting someone who doesn't live where I do. I want to live my life. Somewhere else."

"You're leaving?" Percy sounded like he was about to panic.

Isabelle's anxiety skyrocketed. Her breath was coming and going rapidly, and her fear was overwhelming the annoyance and anger.

"I have to go, Percy."

He was quiet for a moment, studying her face in a way that made her uneasy.

"You can't leave town," Percy murmured, advancing just enough so that there would be no way for her to close her door. Isabelle's fingers tingled to reach for the rifle. But even if she got it, would she really, actually shoot Percy?

It wasn't likely. She wasn't a violent or aggressive woman. She was spirited and energetic and adventurous. Those were completely different things. Shooting someone in the face was beyond the scope of her capabilities.

"I have to leave town, Percy. My ticket, my train ticket, is on the way. I had it sent to me. By the people I will be staying with."

Percy's eyebrows shot up. "So you know where you're going already? This has been your plan for a long time, has it?"

"Not for a long time," Isabelle replied. She didn't have to explain herself to him, she thought. She could do whatever she wanted, whenever she wanted, without consulting him about it. Her fear that he would become violent stopped her from speaking up more. "Just for the past few months. I've been making a plan. I'm bored here. I want to see some of this planet before I get too old or get settled down. So I'm going on an adventure. And I'm sorry, but I don't... I don't need you to be okay with it."

"You can't leave," Percy repeated, pushing his way forward. Before she knew it, he had grabbed her by the arms and was shaking her forward and back. His thick fingers dug into her skin painfully.

"Let me go," she exclaimed, frightened.

"You're supposed to be here with me," he persisted. "We were meant to be together. It's supposed to be you and me. Just you and me. No one else. There's no other woman for me. You must see that. You'll take my heart with you if you leave. Please. You can't go."

Isabelle pulled in her breath and held it. Every muscle in her body was tense.

"I'm leaving, Percy," she said quietly. "Good night."

She stepped back and slammed the door shut before he could react or stop her.

She locked it quickly and turned her back to it, resting her head against it and closing her eyes.

To her astonishment, she heard nothing more, and a few minutes later when she looked, he was gone.

6

"Got another letter, huh?"

Jeremiah looked over his shoulder at the ranch foreman, Brock Landes, when he asked the question. He grinned wide, lifting the paper in his hand and flapping it lightly.

"Yeah," he replied, unable to keep the happiness from his voice. But then, why would he want to? The young woman he'd been corresponding with was ready to come to Texas and get to know him in person. If he'd been asked six weeks ago if he could find a lovely lady to court in such a short amount of time, he would have laughed out a "no" quite loudly. "Isabelle. She's a real nice lady."

"You've been writing to her for that long, have you?"

"Yeah. I sent her a ticket to come here with my last letter."

"Is that so?" Brock looked a little surprised. Jeremiah lifted the hay bale and set it in the back of the wagon. "You tell your mother about this little plan?" He moved the hay bale Jeremiah had lifted up so that it was in the right spot, leaving room for the others.

Jeremiah stopped working, raising his eyebrows at the man. "Why would I want to do something like that? I'm not trying to listen to her nagging me incessantly for information. Besides, she wouldn't approve of this way I'm using. She wouldn't like it. I don't think she would anyway. I think she'd be upset about a Conners finding a woman through a magazine."

"I don't think Mrs. Connelly would approve of any woman you find," Brock replied, shifting his feet, kicking at the stray hay that had come from the bales in loose spots. "I'm actually real surprised she hasn't presented a slew of women to ya, like that lady in the fairy tale. Cinderella."

Jeremiah let out a short laugh. "Cinderella?"

Brock snickered. "Yeah. I mean the prince in that tale, though, ya know. The one who tried that slipper on every foot in the kingdom. His folks had all the women available paraded in front of him, and he got to choose one of 'em. Surprised your mother didn't do that to ya."

Jeremiah snickered, picturing himself walking down a line of women from Hanging Branch and just picking one from them. The imagery made his snicker turn to a full-on laugh. "You're right. Can't believe she didn't do that to me. *Glad* she didn't do that to me."

"You and me both. I don't want my girl to be paraded in front of you."

"I would never... never..." He shook his head, still laughing softly.

"So, what do you know about her?" Brock asked. "All you've said so far is that she's a Southern Belle, right?"

Jeremiah's smile was unwavering. He didn't think about his corresponding pen pal without one plastered to his face.

"She's a Southern Belle, all right. Her name is Isabelle, and it doesn't get more fittin' than that, does it? She likes to sing. Is good at it, I reckon. She says she is."

"Well, that'll be somethin' ya two will have in common then. You can start entertainin' us at church on Sunday."

Jeremiah's heart quickened. He felt his face turning red. He did enjoy singing. There was no doubt about that. But he didn't enjoy doing it for an audience.

"Don't expect me to get into any competitions, Brock. Ain't happening."

Brock harumphed. "Okay, buddy."

"Well, you obviously don't believe me. But I reckon ever since I picked up that letter off my desk and smelled that sweet fragrance coming off it, I was intrigued. She's intelligent, I can tell. And energetic. Probably more so than even I am."

Brock gave him a look. "You're energetic?"

Jeremiah pretended to be affronted. "Yeah. I work all the time. From the time I wake up until I go to bed."

Brock grinned. "I'm teasin' ya. So she's smart and energetic. What else do you know about her? You didn't tell your mother about her, but did ya tell the woman about your mother?"

Jeremiah cleared his throat, looking away from Brock, pulling a cord around the hay bale behind him. He pushed his hands in and grabbed the bale, lifting it and tossing it in the back of the wagon. Brock grabbed it, hauling it backward to the front of the wagon.

"Oops, ya didn't tell her either, huh? And you're just gonna let her brave your mother without warning, huh? I don't think either woman will appreciate that. I understand why you don't want to tell your mother. But I think you better warn Isabelle before she is confronted."

Jeremiah nodded. He'd thought about it and already had a plan. He stopped sorting the hay bales and leaned against the back of the wagon, propping his elbows on the tailgate. Brock stepped forward, took hold of the edge of the wagon, and propelled himself off it, his boots lifting dust in the air on impact with the ground.

"I'm gonna tell her," he said in a reasonable voice, striking a match and touching it to the end of the packed herbs in the pipe he'd pulled from his vest pocket. He shook the match out and took a few puffs of the sweet herbs. After blowing a cloud of smoke, he said, "I actually thought I'd take her to Potter's Creek Restaurant. It's the nicest one in town, don't you think?"

Brock chuckled. "Of the three choices, yeah, I reckon it's the nicest. They're all pretty nice. You could take her to any of 'em. So that's when you're gonna tell her about your mother? Do you know what you should do? You should cook a meal for her.

Send the cook on. Get out the recipe book. Cook up something nice for her. You like to cook, don'tcha?"

Jeremiah stared at the foreman, wondering when Brock had noticed such a subtle thing about him. "I... yeah, I do like to cook. I don't, though. Not much. How'd you even know about that?"

Brock shrugged, turning his eyes to stare down at his boots. "I've been workin' here for some years now, Jeremiah. I've learned some things about you and the rest of your family, not real important stuff maybe, just little things about ya. It's those little things that made me stay with the family all this time."

They were quiet for a moment. Jeremiah's mind strayed to a memory of his father, talking to him about their foreman and how trusted he was. His father had described Brock as one of the strongest men he knew, not just in muscle mass but in character, too.

"Brock, what did you think of my father's stipulation that I had to get married? Do you think he was really that worried that I would never get married?"

"He was worried about it, Jeremiah," Brock confirmed without hesitation. "He talked about it more often than you might think. He didn't understand how a good-looking fella like you didn't have a woman on your arm. He didn't want to push you, but I think when he got sick, it started to weigh on his mind more. I overheard him talking to your mother about it. She was scared by how much it bothered him. She really loved him."

Jeremiah stared at his feet, puffing on the pipe. "I didn't realize that."

"Don't let it weigh on ya too much, Jeremiah," Brock said, slapping one hand on the shorter man's shoulder. "Looks like you've found that woman now. He knows it. Ya know he knows it."

"I hope it works out," Jeremiah replied, his chest tight with apprehension.

"Me, too, buddy. Me too."

7

Isabelle pushed her clothes down in the trunk, trying to pack all the dresses and underthings in one. She'd recruited some boys from town to help her transport the heavy trunks to the train station since there were three of them. Her ticket— the ticket to her freedom, she thought, was sitting in plain sight on the nightstand by her bed.

She was leaving every stick of furniture behind, mostly because it wasn't hers. Granted, she had one or two items in her room she'd bought with her own money, but nearly everything she owned that she didn't wear had been bought with her uncle's money.

Isabelle probably could have taken any objects from the house with her if she wanted. But other than a few personal things, she didn't want to appear greedy. Her aunt and uncle might actually return to the cottage someday. She'd written to them to let them know she was leaving and had received a very encouraging letter from them.

Ever since she received the letter containing the train ticket, Isabelle's heart had been racing. She was anxious the entire night before she was set to go and didn't really get any sleep, deciding she would sleep on the train. She wasn't worried.

Now, the last of her things were packed, and she'd dragged the two larger trunks to the front door. The smaller third one was now packed and ready to go, as well. She took hold of the lid and pulled it over to latch it shut.

Sitting on her bed for the last time, Isabelle glanced around. This had been her home her entire life. After the loss of her parents, she might have experienced a lot of hardship. But she'd been spared, blessed with two loving people who wanted to care for her, show her love and teach her how to be a kind, responsible adult.

It had been a good upbringing. She was independent and unworried about living a fulfilled life since she was confident she could make happen whatever she wanted to happen. It was her life. She was ready to live it to the fullest.

A knock on the door drew her attention. If it was the boys from town who came to fetch the trunks, they were early. Her train wasn't set to leave for another few hours. She'd thought about getting a bit of rest, maybe taking a nap before leaving.

She stood up, and the thought that it might be Percy at the door made her hesitate. It didn't really matter, though. She knew how to handle the man.

Isabelle pulled the front door open to a smiling Margie.

"Well, hello, Margie," she said enthusiastically. "What are you doing here?"

"I couldn't let you leave without bringing you a few things," Margie replied, rushing past her without waiting for an invitation to come in. It was fine with Isabelle, though, and Margie knew that which was probably why she did it.

Isabelle looked down at the basket her friend was holding. It was rectangular and had two lids that lifted in the opposite direction of each other.

She set the basket down and stood still for a moment. Isabelle almost didn't have time to wonder what Margie was doing. Her friend suddenly looked up, tears standing in her eyes.

"I... I couldn't let you go without saying good-bye," she whispered.

Isabelle's heart melted for her friend. She crossed the room to Margie quickly, pulling the woman into a hug. "Surely you won't miss me that much," she laughed softly.

"Don't be ridiculous," Margie said abruptly, putting her hands up to her face and wiping under her eyes. Isabelle could see by the redness of her face she'd been crying. She looked like she was on the verge again. Isabelle pulled her into another warm hug, which Margie returned.

"I'm going to miss you, too, Margie," she said. "I promise I'll come back someday and see you again. This man I'm marrying is supposed to be very wealthy. If he's as kind and generous as I'm praying he is, he will give me enough money to visit sometimes. Especially if my aunt and uncle come back."

Margie seemed to recover quickly from her distress, giving Isabelle a hopeful look. "You think he will be? Does he sound like he would be like that in his letters?"

Isabelle nodded, pulling back so Margie could spread open the two lids of the basket. She was curious to see what goodies her friend had brought her.

"Yes. He really does seem to be..." She pulled in a deep breath, moving to the chair of the table and sliding into it comfortably. She really had been blessed, she thought, looking around. Her aunt and uncle had taken good care of her. "I can't really tell, though. Not yet, you know. I can only pray I'm judging him correctly."

Margie looked a lot more confident than she had when she came in. Isabelle was a little surprised by her friend's reaction, but the more she thought about Margie, the more she understood why there had been such a dramatic reaction.

Berkenshire wasn't the smallest Virginia city, but it wasn't one of the largest by far. She tried to think of another woman in their town that Margie spent time with as often as Isabelle did.

There was no one. Margie wasn't married and worked in the family business. Isabelle was privy to every occasion a man had shown interest in her friend. She'd been there when Margie left school to start working in the business after graduating from the highest grade in school. She'd even been in the house when Margie's little sister had been born, though the memory was well-faded from the years that stretched between then and now.

She refused to think she was Margie's only

friend. Surely there was at least one or two other women in town, regardless of age, who considered Margie more than just an acquaintance or a fellow resident of Berkenshire.

Isabelle watched Margie pulling various items up and showing them to her, such as a jar of dressing Margie had made herself, grapes, apples, oranges, and potatoes for food items. It wasn't until Margie pulled from the basket a large sketchbook and some charcoal sticks in a package lined with gold trimming that Isabelle felt the weight her leaving would have on Margie.

"Oh, Margie. Thank you so much for this. I didn't expect any kind of present. But you know I will treasure this, and I'll try to improve on my art skills enough to draw you sketches of what I see when I get to Texas."

Margie's eyes went soft. She took one of Isabelle's hands in hers. "You won't forget about me? You promise?"

Isabelle chuckled. "Of course I won't forget about you. I plan to start sketching as soon as I get there. Every time I start drawing and using this book and these sticks, I'll be thinking of you the whole time."

Margie laughed with her. Isabelle didn't miss the

unmistakable sadness that came through that laughter.

"I'm so happy for you, Isabelle," her friend said, looking directly into her eyes. "I want you to know that. I think it will be very lonely for me here without you. I can't make a friend and have the years of experience I have with you. I know you so well. I won't make another friend like you easily."

Isabelle was amused and flattered by the woman's attention. She tilted her head to the side, giving Margie a kind smile. "You're the one who pointed me to the ads in the first place."

Margie nodded, raising her eyebrows. "A mistake I'll likely regret the rest of my life."

Isabelle was relieved when Margie laughed again.

"I will live, honey. I'm just going to miss you, that's all. I'm truly happy for you. I truly, truly am."

8

Ten minutes after Margie left, Isabelle stood at the front door, watching for the boys to come from town to help her with her luggage. She was still nervous and anxious to get on the road. Her train was still an hour from coming.

The clock in the living room of the cottage told her it was time for them to arrive, and she would have quickly become anxious if she didn't see some dust in the distance, rising up from a rider coming toward the cottage. In a few moments, the boys would come around the corner, and she would see it was them. She hoped it was them.

She was cutting it close enough already.

When the rider turned the corner, her heart plummeted into her stomach, and all the air went out of her lungs. She hurried back into her house and started to drag the trunks out. One of the larger trunks was mostly heavy because of the bulkiness of the thing itself. It contained dresses, which didn't weigh much at all.

The other large one was heavier. She had put mementos and other things she wanted to keep that weren't necessarily clothing items. Her personal items had gone into the smaller of the three trunks. She could lift the smallest one with ease. The one containing dresses was difficult to handle. This one —with so many other things inside it than cloth— was darn near impossible for her to pick up. Sliding it was difficult, too.

She didn't acknowledge Percy when he got close to the cottage. She had to get the buggy ready. The boys weren't there yet. They'd have to show up very soon to make it in time for her not to be late for the scheduled train. She had to leave very, very soon.

"You don't have to do that, Isabelle," Percy said, sliding out of the saddle. He stalked toward her as if he was going to stop what she was doing. She skill- fully dodged him and swung around to face him once she was at the top of the short steps to her porch.

"I will do what I have to do, Percy. What are you

doing here? I don't remember asking you to come. I'm waiting for the boys I hired from town to come and help me with my trunks. They must be running late, so I have to take matters into my own hands."

Percy's face suddenly looked pinched. "They aren't coming. I told them I was going to change your mind. And that's what I've come here to do."

Isabelle's chest tightened with apprehension. There was no way she would allow this man to tell her what to do with her life. He had gotten physical with her several times since she told him she was leaving, grabbing her when she passed him on the street, pulling her into alleyways to "have a discussion." She was terrified of him but did her best not to show it. She was grateful for the long sleeves she wore. Even if she had short sleeves to wear, she wouldn't. She wasn't about to show the finger marks and hand bruises from the grip of his hands.

"I can't stay, Percy." She felt like she'd said that a thousand times over the last two months. "I have plans for my life, and they don't include Berkenshire. In fact, they don't even include Virginia. Now please, you have to leave."

It wasn't until she turned around to grab the closest handle of the trunk nearest her that what he said processed through her mind. She turned slowly, glaring at him.

"Did you say you told them not to come? *You told them not to come and help me?*"

"I need to make you understand the error of your ways, Isabelle."

Isabelle closed her eyes, fury rising up in her gut. She tried to level it off and keep herself under control.

"I love you, Isabelle. I need you to see that. Please."

Isabelle blinked at him over her shoulder. She'd already placed both hands on the handle of the heaviest trunk. She was preparing to pull it as hard as she could. Her buggy could fit the three trunks. It fit several people and had a trundle compartment in the back. Surely that was enough room. She could picture it in her mind. She knew exactly how she would arrange it.

"You had no right to interfere in my business, Percy. I've got a good mind to tell your father what a cad you've been to me. How you won't leave me alone and think I'm your property. I'm never have been and am not now someone's property. Do you understand that?"

Percy chuckled. "I know you are a feisty little filly, that's for sure."

To her utter surprise and disgust, he came up on the porch and leaned over her from behind, his arms beside hers, his hands over hers as he grasped at the same handle of the trunk.

Isabelle recoiled, the shock of feeling his body pressed against hers making her feel repulsed.

"What are you doing?" she nearly shrieked, her skin crawling with disgust.

"I'm tryin' to help."

The overwhelming stench of alcohol on his breath made Isabelle gag. She slid out from under him and stepped away, her wide eyes glaring at him.

"How dare you, sir. You do not have the right to touch me like that. Please. I need you to leave. At once,"

"I was jus' tryin' to help." For the first time, she noticed his slurring words and his drooping eyes. She hadn't noticed before because she consciously avoided knowing too much about the man.

"I don't want you to touch me. I don't want you to help me. I am going to be late for my train, and I want to go now. You need to leave me this instant. I don't want your help. Go. Go,"

She lifted one arm and pointed with a violence

that made her arm hurt at her shoulder because she was stabbing the air so hard with one finger.

"Get off my property. Get off."

"This isn't technically your property, you know," Percy said with a smirk.

Isabelle had had enough. She stepped toward him, despite the urge to turn and run in the opposite direction. She marched over to him and grabbed him by the front of his vest, which was as high up as she could reach. If she was a tall man like him, she would have grabbed him by his collar.

Isabelle realized taking his vest the way she had wouldn't have the same impact as it would have if she'd grabbed his collar. So she adjusted what she would normally have done and shoved him to the side as hard as he could.

Percy wobbled at the top of the short staircase for a moment or two before getting his balance by grabbing a rail. She turned swiftly, and with all her strength, she yanked on the handle of the smallest trunk. It lifted up in the air and made straight for Percy's head. He had no time to react.

Isabelle decided later, when replaying it in her mind, the buckle of the trunk—one of the two buckles on that side—must have clocked him a good one in the head. It was lights out for Percy.

Isabelle grabbed the handle in a tighter grip and ran down the stairs with it. She flung it up in the back seat of the four-person buggy. One of the other large trunks would fit in the passenger seat. The third and final trunk would be pushed into the trundle bed of the vehicle.

She was tremendously relieved when Percy didn't get back up. She pulled a small mirror from her bag, moved to where he was, and held it in front of his face. She could see his breath fogging the looking glass and fanned herself in relief.

She slid the small mirror into her bag and pulled the purse all the way around her shoulder. If she moved fast, she could get her trunks in the buggy and get to the train station before he woke up.

9

———

Jeremiah adjusted his hat as he got close to the train station. He furrowed his brow, wondering if the train had come early or if his watch was wrong. The place was teeming with people, and the train was sitting in the station. How long had it been there?

He jumped out of the buggy as soon as he made it to the lot and found a spot to leave it. He jogged to the platform and leaped up onto it, surpassing the three steps there for his convenience.

Jeremiah slid his eyes through the crowd, looking for a woman with green eyes, red hair, and the clothes of someone from the south.

He spotted her standing near the door of the station, looking at people as they passed by. She had a pleasant look on her face, not worried or stressed, which pleased him. That said a lot to him when he was obviously late getting there to pick her up.

"Excuse me," he said, approaching her. Her green eyes turned to him. A wash of relief mixed with attraction slid through him. "You are Isabelle Lawton? From Virginia?"

She smiled wide, showing a row of almost perfect teeth on top. One of her upper teeth in the front was slightly crooked. Something about that tiny flaw made Jeremiah's heart skip a beat.

"Hello," she said, holding out one gloved hand. "I am Isabelle. You're Jeremiah, I take it?"

"I am. I'm really glad to meet you. I'm so sorry for being late. Please accept my heartfelt apology."

Isabelle giggled. "Don't apologize. The train was a little early. We've only been here about five minutes."

Jeremiah looked around them. "We?"

She shook her head. "Oh, I just mean myself and my fellow passengers. It was an interesting ride. There were so many different types of people on board. I've never been out of Berkenshire like I told you in my letter. It's so interesting to meet all kinds of people and see things you've never seen before.

That's what I've been craving for so long now. So long."

She sighed, looking from left to right, taking in everything around them.

He instantly liked her. She was bubbly and charming. Her energy was contagious. And to top it all off, she was extremely pretty. She had a wonderful figure in the dark green dress she was wearing. Her eyes sparkled with animation.

"Do you have luggage?"

Isabelle nodded, her eyes widening. He almost laughed out loud when she started talking excitedly, "Oh yes, I certainly do. I had to put them myself into my buggy and get someone to take my buggy back to my aunt and uncle's. You should have seen me struggling. I got the boys at the train station, the attendants, I got them to get them from my buggy for me. I did think ahead, though. Don't you go thinking I didn't. I went and hired two boys to come to help me. But there's a man in Berkenshire who was just constantly worrying and annoying me. He told them he was going to help me. But by golly, I didn't want him helping me. I wanted the boys I paid for. I didn't want him to help me, so I—"

She stopped abruptly, her cheeks heating slightly. Her eyes lifted up, and she stared into space for a moment. He could tell she was remembering. He wished he knew what she was seeing in her mind. On the outside, she looked sweet and pretty. Her smile was genuine.

"I fear I'm rambling," she said abruptly. "I... I apologize."

He shook his head. "No, don't. I rather enjoy listening to you. But let's go in and get your bags. I've got the buggy with me. I'm sure there will be plenty of room."

She grinned sweetly. "I hope so. I have two large trunks and one small one. You have to have a compartment in the back to get all three at once."

Jeremiah wiggled his eyebrows. "We are in luck then."

Ten minutes later, they were riding away from the station, basking in the bright sun above. The roads were fairly smooth, having been driven over many, many times. Jeremiah described his hometown to her.

"I can see why it's called Hanging Branch," she said, her voice gentle. He glanced at her, admiring the way her curious eyes swept over the land as they rode along. She was taking in the many Willow trees that lined both sides of the road. They were coming up on the main street bridge, which Jeremiah had always thought was a beautiful area. He was looking forward to her reaction to seeing the beauty of the ancient bridge.

It was made of large blocks of stone and stretched in an arch over the river. The willow trees were on both sides of the water, which had sparkling clear water that allowed the viewer to see all the way to the bottom, where colorful rocks lined the riverbed.

"This is Main Street Bridge," he said as they got closer, flipping his eyes to her repeatedly to see her face. He loved seeing her eyes open wide, her eyebrows raising up.

"Oh my,"

"It's also known as Butterfly Bridge," Jeremiah went on, using a soft, gentle tone. "During certain times of the day and year, when the weather and the conditions are just right, flocks of butterflies will flitter around. And if you stop and approach a swarm of butterflies, a lot of them will land on you. You can stretch your arms out to the sides and be covered in them for at least a minute or so before they all fly away."

Isabelle sucked in her breath and held it. He was pleased and smiled.

"I've had that happen to me at least a dozen

times over the years. I was born and raised here, you know."

"I know," she replied softly. "I hope I will have the opportunity to have that happen to me. It sounds lovely and fascinating. Oh, I would like that so much. There's nowhere like that in Berkenshire. That's not to say it isn't beautiful in Virginia. I must say there are more green hills and tall mountains there. Our little valley town was surrounded on all four sides by mountains. The only time that didn't serve us well was when it rained too much. The flooding was something bad. But we prepared for it. That was the key, you know. If you prepare well enough for some kind of disaster, you can usually survive it with just a little damage, instead of so much that you have to move."

"You didn't have to do that, did you?"

"No, I didn't," Isabelle replied to his question.

"I'm glad to hear that. You lived in that little cottage of yours until now, didn't you?"

She nodded. "I did. You know, it wasn't a very small cottage, really. There were plenty of rooms, and the rooms were big. My aunt and uncle, well, I guess they thought they would have one or two children, and if they had more, they would move. But they ended up not having any children of their own.

I suppose that's why they were so quick to take care of me. I was the only child they would ever raise."

As she continued talking, Jeremiah watched her, fascinated by her energy. He didn't foresee having any trouble falling in love with this woman. He would have to be careful not to fall for her too quickly. He wanted to know as much about her as he could. He wanted to make the right decision.

Just listening to her, though, Jeremiah was sure of one thing. He would never be bored.

10

"So tell me more about your singing," Isabelle said, licking a bit of jelly off her finger and smiling at him.

Since her arrival, the two had talked almost non-stop, trading humorous stories about their childhoods. They'd decided to test each other's cooking skills after playfully teasing about how good they were.

"I don't want to talk about singing right now," Jeremiah replied bluntly. She'd already gotten used to that from him, as he did it quite often. She could tell by his quiet demeanor he wasn't being rude—wasn't intending to be, anyway. "I want to talk about what you are doing to that sausage."

Isabelle was impressed by Jeremiah's kitchen. He

had a pantry that was stocked with dried goods, a cellar for cold storage, a large icebox to keep things cold, and a wide variety of herbs and spices in small bottles. Some she had never heard of.

"I'm just adding a bit of this jelly," she replied. "You'd be surprised what it does to the taste, adding something so sweet to the meat."

He lifted one eyebrow, his gaze still on the sausage in the pan. "I'm interested to find out," he continued. "I must admit, it smells good."

"You'll love it. I just know it."

Isabelle moved the sausage around in the pan, thinking about their stop at the butcher for fresh meat. Jeremiah confessed to a sweet tooth sometime in their travel to the ranch, and she hadn't forgotten that. Some time ago, she had read of a special sweet snack she could make with molasses. She'd made a mental note to make that for him.

She was extremely pleased with how things were turning out. This man was not only quite good-looking, but he was also strong in both body and mind. He would be able to protect her, should she need protecting. She could also look forward to having interesting conversations with him because he was obviously an intelligent man.

So far, she'd seen no flaws in him. There had to be something.

Her thoughts made her giggle. She was glad she was facing the stove, hovering over the pan. He couldn't see her face.

"If you decide to stay here," Jeremiah said, backing away from the stove, practically forcing her to turn and look at him, "I want you to know you won't have to cook. I know you might *want* to cook and if you do, please, go right ahead. You can get fresh ingredients whenever you want. I'll give you a purse. An allowance."

Isabelle lifted her eyebrows, turning all the way around and moving slightly to the side so she could lean against the counter behind her. "Do you think I will want to leave?" she asked. She tried to ask the question soberly without letting her thoughts invade her voice. She wasn't sure she had succeeded. Everything was going so well so far. They were getting along. She was so impressed with him overall. She hooped she was making a good impression on him.

He seemed so relaxed, even with the pointed question being lobbed at him.

He shrugged, further proving his relaxation.

"I want you to know that it's completely up to

you. I don't want you to stay where you don't want to be."

"You're not going to try to get me to stay? How will I know if you want me here?"

He chuckled, which was not the reaction Isabelle was expecting. But when he met her eyes, she knew he wasn't laughing at her questions in any way.

"I think we are doing well together for just having met," he said. "Even if we did correspond through the mail for over a month. We're still strangers, aren't we?"

"No," she replied, shaking her head. "We were strangers when we first started corresponding." She gave him a warm smile. "Now we are friends. And I'm here to see if we want to make that friendship something more. Right?"

Jeremiah's grin grew gradually as she spoke. She liked how animated his expressions were. It wasn't very hard to see what he was thinking. He was probably terrible at poker.

She giggled behind her hand, and his brown eyebrows shot up, an amused look on his face.

"What's funny?" he asked.

Isabelle didn't turn away from him. She enjoyed just gazing at him. "I want to stay, Jeremiah. If you want me to leave at any point—if it turns out we don't really get along as well as we seem to right now, I'll go. My aunt and uncle will take care of me no matter what happens. They will see that I'm safe. But as of right now, I would very much like to stay and give it a go."

She adored the smile he gave her.

"I feel the same way. If, for some ungodly reason, we start arguing a lot and not getting along, one of us can back out. Correct?"

"That's correct," Isabelle replied, nodding curtly.

"But right now, we both really want to continue this evening with a nice dinner cooked by our own hands, right?"

Isabelle didn't tell him her meals were always cooked by her own hands. She'd inherited a cottage from her aunt and uncle. Surely he didn't think she employed a cook.

"That's right," was her response. There was no need to bring up irrelevant additions like pointing out the disparity in their wealth and status. "I must say you are one of the easiest going ranchers I've ever met."

He gave her a puzzled look. "You've met a lot of ranchers?"

"Well, they do have such things in Virginia," she

retorted before grinning wide, "still, yes, you are the first one I've met."

"I think you'll find you were right regardless."

They both laughed.

THEY WERE SEATED at an elegant table with enough chairs to seat a decent-sized dinner party. It was covered by a white cloth adorned with threads of gold making shapes and swirls in the fabric. The plates were larger than Isabelle was used to. Although the table was long and had two chairs on either end, when they went in, Jeremiah pulled out one of the side chairs, indicating that's where he wanted her to sit.

She'd sat with just a bit of confusion and watched in astonishment as Jeremiah set the table and brought their food to the table. That's when she'd noticed the larger than normal plates. The centerpiece was masterful, a large gold vase with swooping side handles and pretty flowers stuffed into it, drooping over the sides.

Isabelle thought it was beautiful.

"It's time to try our masterpieces," Jeremiah announced, setting one tray down in front of her and one in front of him. Her sausage, potato, and peppers meal was taught to her by her aunt. He said he got his steak and potatoes recipe from one of his cook's handwritten book of recipes.

He served them both, and she stared down at the delicious-looking meat and potatoes on her plate.

"I think we forgot to make biscuits or toast. We should have a bread with this, shouldn't we?"

Jeremiah chuckled, sitting at his place at the head of the table. He grinned at her, holding his fork in one hand and pointed at the ceiling and his knife in the other, the way a small child might do.

"No time for baking now. You ready?"

She took up her utensils the same way and grinned wide, scrunching her eyes at him.

"I'm ready."

"When I say go. Ready. Set."

Jeremiah never got to say the last word.

His mouth was open, and it was about to come out when the door of the dining room swung open, and a woman walked in, followed by one of the most beautiful ladies Isabelle had ever seen. She immediately saw a resemblance between Jeremiah and the older woman leading the younger one in.

"Mother?"

Isabelle's eyes swerved to Jeremiah, hearing

astonishment in his voice. She saw his eyes on the younger woman. His face seemed suspicious.

"Who is this?" he asked.

The older woman settled her eyes on Isabelle.

"Who is this?"

Isabelle could not have felt more uncomfortable than she did at that moment. For the first time since she'd arrived in Low Branch, Texas, she felt unwelcome.

11

Jeremiah was mortified to see the beautiful woman step in behind his mother. He immediately knew what had happened. He didn't blame his mother. Of course she was just trying to help. But he was sure she'd chosen that woman from a pool of wealthy, influential families and would immediately reject someone with Isabelle's background and current status.

He stood up, glancing at Isabelle, who looked like she wanted to crawl in a hole and die.

"Mother, we need to talk." Jeremiah moved away from the table quickly, holding out one hand. He was intending on grabbing her elbow and steering her toward the door so they could talk outside.

As soon as he was close enough, she jerked her arm away, glaring at him.

"What have you done? Who is this? Tell me what's going on."

Jeremiah was used to his mother's dramatic behavior, and seeing it on full display in front of Isabelle filled him with guilt because he had never gotten around to warning Isabelle about Clarice. Sometimes it was impossible for him not to think of the woman who birthed him by her first name. She was, on the one hand, rigid and stern and, on the other hand, overly dramatic about everything. She acted like she was the queen of the manor ninety-nine percent of the time.

"I met someone and have been conversing with her for some time now. I invited her over for dinner."

He looked over his shoulder, his eyes landing on Isabelle and locking with hers. She didn't look happy. His heart ached. The only reason he hadn't warned her about his mother was that they had been getting along so well that he'd forgotten. His mother hadn't shown her face the entire day, even before he went to the train station that afternoon.

"Well, I have found you the wife you have been seeking." She stepped back and held out her hands in the young woman's direction as if she was on display. "This is Victoriana Wilson. You might remember her father, the barrister in Fort Sunney? I found out through him that she was interested in you. So here she is. Your problems are solved."

Jeremiah didn't know how to feel. She was only trying to help. He knew that. But she also knew that if he didn't marry and Uncle Daniel took control, she wouldn't be the queen of the manor anymore. Not at all. That privilege would fall to someone else, someone who hadn't lived at the ranch in that grand house for most of their adult life.

Not to mention the money would be gone.

"We need to speak outside," Jeremiah lowered his voice to say the words, reaching out and successfully grasping her elbow. He pulled her a little roughly toward the door, and she nearly stumbled. She righted herself, her cheeks flushing, and hurried toward the door, her back to the other women.

Jeremiah lifted one hand to Victoriana and moved it to Isabelle. "I'll be right back. Please allow me to apologize to you both. This was just..." He ran out of appropriate words and sucked in a sharp breath, shaking his head. "I'll be right back. Please, Victoriana, have a seat."

She smiled brightly at him. His first thought was that she had a kind face. She was a little too late for what she was there for, but that didn't make her a bad person, did it?

"Of course," she said, taking a step toward him. "I'll… I'll just sit down over there." She gestured with her purse at the table where Isabelle was watching the entire situation unfold with a stony face.

Jeremiah couldn't possibly imagine how she was feeling right then. He didn't want to think about it. One thing at a time, he told himself. Right now, he needed to scold his mother for not consulting him.

He stepped outside to see his mother standing by the railing around the porch, staring out in the distance. Her arms were crossed over her chest. As soon as his boots hit the wood flooring, she spun around to show him how deep her frown was.

"What have you done, Jeremiah?" she asked. Her arms unfolded, and she flailed them around, gesturing wildly. "How could you possibly have been conversing with this woman for some time now? I don't even know her. I know a lot of people, son. I know a lot. I know people in the surrounding coun-ties almost as well as the ones who live right here in Low Branch. And I don't. Know. Her. Now tell me where you found her?"

Jeremiah was offended by the way she said he

found her as if she was some stray animal he'd found in a ravine somewhere, injured and alone.

"I have been corresponding with her through the mail. She is from Virginia. A small town in Virginia. I didn't tell you about the letters we were sending because I knew you'd have this kind of reaction. I'm hoping she will marry me. I only have a month left. A month and a week. I don't want to start getting to know someone new, even if it is a lovely-looking young woman."

He hated the spark of hope he saw in her eyes.

"Mother, don't do this." He had to harden his voice. "You are going to make one of these young ladies very unhappy if you continue this. I don't want to start new. I like Isabelle. She and I have a lot in common. She is a good-looking woman and seems to be strong and happy to be alive. I want to explore the possibilities with her."

"I want you to consider Victoriana," his mother said. "You haven't asked the woman to marry you yet, have you? You aren't formally engaged, are you?"

Jeremiah was taken aback. She expected him to ask Isabelle to let him make a choice after getting to know Victoriana? If he was a woman, he would slap himself across the face and never see himself again.

"I can't ask Isabelle to let me make a decision like that. She will surely leave me."

"Then she doesn't really care about your happiness," the woman huffed. Jeremiah tried hard to understand her line of thinking.

"What are you talking about?" he asked harshly.

"If she cares about you like you think she does, she will let you have a chance to decide. She will understand that you need and deserve what's best for you. If that's Vicky, then that's Vicky. If she truly cares, who is she to stand in your way? This is what she would be thinking."

"Isabelle doesn't deserve this. She's traveled a long way to be with me."

His mother huffed, holding her nose up high in the air. "All the more reason for her to let you make the decision. If she thinks she will win your heart, she should stay and fight for you and find out if she is right. If not, she should accept her fate."

"I don't believe you, mother," Jeremiah murmured, shaking his head. "You've put me in an impossible position. How could you do this?"

"I was looking out for you, son," she responded in a haughty voice he recognized. She reserved that tone for people she felt were less than her, not as intelligent, not as intuitive. It wasn't the first time he'd heard that tone. His father had heard it more than anyone else.

Frankly, Jeremiah didn't know how he put up with it for so many years.

"You knew your father's concern about getting you married. You know he would approve of my choice over yours. That is an obvious fact."

Frustration filled Jeremiah. He lifted his hands in the air and shook his head.

"I'm done with this conversation," he said firmly. "We will talk about it later. I want to help Isabelle get settled in. She doesn't have a home here, and I'm giving her one until things are sorted out. Please accept her and make her feel welcome and comfortable even if it's the last thing you want to do."

12

Isabelle stared at the woman as she walked to the table, but when Victoriana's eyes moved to her, she averted her own and studied her fingers. She'd never been in a situation like that. She prided herself on being an understanding person and didn't want to feel anger or resentment toward the woman who'd come in with Jeremiah's mother. After all, it wasn't her fault. Any more than it was Isabelle's fault.

Anger wasn't really what she was experiencing anyway. She was insecure. She had never questioned her outer appearance before, not really. She was satisfied with the features on her face and content with the way one side of her lips stretched higher than the other when she smiled. She was happy with the body she was given by the Lord and enjoyed having a head of full wavy red hair. Her eyes were no less but no more than average.

The woman sitting across from her was stunning. She seemed to have the perfect face, narrow eyes, long, dark lashes, slender features, and the perfect smile.

Isabelle lifted her gaze and saw the woman was still looking at her.

"Hello," she said as soon as she saw Isabelle was looking at her. "I'm sorry this has happened."

Isabelle was typically a friendly, outgoing person. It was the first time in her life she didn't know how to respond. Was this woman trying to make friends with her? Did she misunderstand the circumstances that were currently going on?

"Hello," she responded blandly. "I'm sorry, too."

"I didn't know Jeremiah already had someone he was speaking to and seeing socially. How long have you been here?"

Isabelle felt a tingle of apprehension. She'd only arrived that day. She didn't have any real seniority in the situation. What was one afternoon and a few letters? It probably didn't amount to much in the long run.

She hoped she wasn't blushing but had a feeling her cheeks were hot for a reason.

"I arrived today on a train from Virginia."

Victoriana gazed at her, genuine surprise on her face. "You came all this way from Virginia to see Jeremiah? That's a long way."

She spoke in such a breathless way, so soft and gentle. Isabelle had a hard time continuing to be upset with her. She thought it best to send her ire toward the actual target where they belonged. That would be Jeremiah's mother.

And the more she thought about it, the more she wondered what Jeremiah was thinking. Why hadn't he told her about the older woman and how controlling she seemed to be? Why didn't he warn her what she might be getting into? He obviously had said nothing about her to his mother. Was he ashamed of the ad he'd put in the magazine?

Her chest tightened with anxiety and anger. She felt taken advantage of. She was so close to having exactly the life she wanted with a man who seemed completely compatible with her.

And right off the bat—it was teetering on disaster. She sighed.

"It *is* a long way," she admitted, nodding. "And I

was very much looking forward to eating this dinner with Jeremiah. Now I fear it will get cold and taste horrible."

Victoriana turned to the table and eyed the food that was indeed getting colder by the moment.

"Well, I am not hungry," she mentioned amiably. "So if you are and you want to go ahead, I won't be offended."

Isabelle blinked at the woman. She wished Victoriana wasn't so nice. It made it hard to be angry.

"I shouldn't," she said, ashamed to admit at least fifty percent of her really wanted to eat the steak dinner he'd prepared for her. It had probably sat just long enough to be the perfect eating temperature. She eyed it hungrily. It had been a long, arduous day.

Isabelle looked back at Victoriana. "You sure you don't mind? I don't want to..." She thought twice about it when her hand jerked toward the fork leaning on the side of her plate.

She couldn't be eating when Jeremiah came back in with his mother. That would make her look terrible. She was sure of it.

The next moment, she was suspicious that Victoriana had tried to set her up to look bad in front of Jeremiah's mother. Her feelings of friendliness toward the woman soured. She couldn't help it when her face screwed up, and she turned away from the woman.

Isabelle lifted from the chair and strolled across the room to the window as casually as she could. She crossed her arms over her chest, hugging herself tightly.

"I can't be eating when he comes back in, even if the meal he made specifically for me gets cold."

"It doesn't have to," Victoriana responded. Isabelle turned her head to look back at the other young woman as she stood up and leaned over to place a large tray lid over Isabelle's plate. "It will still cool off, but at least it won't get any bugs on it, and the heat will stay in for a little longer. Perhaps you'll be able to eat it after all."

Isabelle felt a twinge of gratitude. "Best to put one over his plate, too."

Victoriana nodded, turning to place a second lid over his. "Looks like there are two lids. You must have made each other dinner."

Isabelle was impressed with Victoriana's intuitiveness. "Yes, we did."

"Well, it looks and smells wonderful. I'm sorry

my intrusion interrupted your good time. I'll see about leaving when Clarice comes back in."

Clarice.

Isabelle ran the name through her mind several times. It sounded cold and calculating to her. She was willing to bet that was how Clarice was, too. Cold and calculating.

Just look at what she'd done to Isabelle's hope for the future.

"You'll do no such thing, Victoriana Wilson."

Both women turned when Clarice's voice rang sharply in the air. Isabelle felt a little sick to her stomach. "You're going to stay right here with us in the guest room that has already been made up and ready." The older woman turned to Jeremiah. "I was surprised and pleased to hear you tell Lucy to get it set up, Jeremiah. Now I see you had your own plans."

"That room is for Isabelle," Jeremiah retorted bluntly. He never took his eyes from his mother. Isabelle was surprised and impressed with the way he was handling himself against what appeared to be quite a formidable woman. "There are other rooms we can make up."

"No, there are not," Clarice snapped.

Isabelle was beginning to feel a great deal of

resentment toward Clarice. This was not the way she wanted to start a relationship with the mother of the man she wanted to marry. She'd already decided Jeremiah was perfect for her. This snafu would be resolved, and Victoriana would leave, and they would live happily ever after.

Isabelle fought an audible snort at her thoughts. Clarice was going to be trouble. There was no doubt of that.

"It will take too long to set up another room. Your friend here will have to go to the boarding house in town."

Isabelle's heart sank. Victoriana would be living on the same premises as Jeremiah, but she wouldn't? The thought devastated her.

"No, Mother," Jeremiah replied, bringing some hope to Isabelle's heart. "She's not going to do that. She's going to stay in the bungalow by the creek."

Isabelle didn't think she'd ever heard of a place that sounded more lovely. She raised her eyebrows, ignoring the look of disdain on his mother's face. "Bungalow by the creek?" she repeated back to him.

When he turned to face her, she saw a look of relief flood his face. He must have seen the keen interest she had in seeing this bungalow.

"Yes," he replied enthusiastically. "It's quite

lovely. You'll have all the privacy you want. I'll take you down there right now." He held out his arm to her, and she crossed the room quickly to take it. She didn't miss the way his mother looked at them. She looked disgusted.

The look on Victoriana's face was completely the opposite.

She looked delighted.

13

"How can I possibly apologize enough for my mother's behavior?" Jeremiah's heart ached. One day. Really it was less than one day he'd had with Isabelle. The best half-day of his life so far. If he was able to continue a relationship with Isabelle, he felt like he had a chance at having a bunch more.

Life without her would be miserable now. How could any other woman possibly make him feel the way Isabelle did in just a few short hours?

"You aren't responsible for what your mother does," Isabelle responded in a voice that Jeremiah hoped was forgiving. "But it seems you didn't tell her anything about me. Why wouldn't you? Are you ashamed of how we met?"

Jeremiah lifted his eyebrows and drew in a deep breath. Shaking his head, he responded after thinking just a moment about the right way to say it.

"It isn't that I'm ashamed of it," he said. "It's that *she* would be. She would berate the process and make it seem like we're doing something unnatural. She wants things to be her way and only her way. She won't accept anything else."

Isabelle was quiet for a moment as they walked. He glanced at her to see that she was taking in the scenery around her. He did the same, realizing that he very often overlooked the beauty of his home. His gardener was very good at his job. Jeremiah made a mental note to raise his pay.

"Do you like what you see?" he asked quietly, hoping to change the topic of conversation.

"It's beautiful, Jeremiah," she replied, her voice breathless. "I could live very happily here. It's really beyond words."

Jeremiah thought that was a wonderful way to describe his home. "My father worked hard on this property. He was dedicated to it. Our foreman does most of the ranch work. My father was the businessman and continued to do that when he became ill. When he died, the rights to the land and property will all come to me as long as I'm married within the three months of the will reading." He looked at her to see if she remembered. "I wrote you about it early on."

She returned his gaze, nodding. "Yes, I remember. I understand why your mother felt the need to do what she did. But I don't understand why you... why you didn't tell her what you were doing, well, I guess I do understand. I just wish it wasn't like that. I must say I didn't expect to come all this way to be faced with competition."

Her voice drifted off. Jeremiah had a feeling he knew what she was thinking.

"Victoriana is a beautiful woman," he admitted and hurried to add, "but, Isabelle, I wrote to you with the sole purpose of finding out if you would be a good wife. When I told you the stipulation of the will, and you responded that you understood and were willing to take a chance on me, I knew I'd found a good woman. Now that you're here, I'm certain we can make this work if we fight for it. My mother is a formidable opponent, but she's never come up against me in the game of love. She might beat me every now and then at chess, but this is one thing she won't be able to win. It's my heart. It's my life. It's my feelings. I'm ashamed that you have been sent out here, and I hope you don't feel banished from the house. My mother wouldn't want you to feel that way either."

Isabelle's eyes darted to his face. She looked surprised.

He was dismayed. She was going to get such a bad impression of his mother. He hated that. She wasn't terribly bad. She wasn't a discouraging or abusive mother who called him names and made him feel worthless. Quite to the contrary, Clarice had doted on her boy, attempting to drill into his head how much better he was than "normal" society.

Jeremiah just wasn't an arrogant man. He was naturally humble, realizing his faults and trying to do the best he could every day to be a gentleman, a hard worker, and a good friend.

His mother was just overly dramatic and put on airs. It was her personality. She wasn't mean. She was haughty.

"Please don't think too much ill of my mother," he said, keeping his voice down instinctively. It wasn't like she would hear him talking about her. She probably knew instinctively that they were anyway. "She isn't as selfish as she seems. She tries to be controlling, but the truth is she was always under the thumb of my father."

The more Jeremiah spoke, the more he began to

realize the man he'd thought was his father was much different than he'd believed. Ever since his death, Jeremiah had heard things he'd never heard before. The hard way his father had treated the people that worked for him. The subtle talk of the house staff when they didn't know Jeremiah was around to hear. Not to mention the stipulation he'd left for Jeremiah in his will. Perhaps he thought he was doing the right thing.

"He was a man who was in control of everything in his life. He got up at the same time every morning. He had the same routine to start the day and one to end the day. He never changed that routine either." He hesitated. "I loved him. Please don't get me wrong. I wanted to be just like him. I thought it was so blessed to have everything together all the time. How can one man just automatically have all the answers?"

Jeremiah's heart ached. He could hear his father's booming voice in his mind. Barking orders at the ranch hands like Brock wasn't even there. Changing the schedule to suit what he wanted, not knowing that when he left the area, the ranch hands asked Brock what to do, and he made the final decisions.

He wondered why he had never realized any of that before.

Isabelle hadn't said anything. He looked down at her to see the expression of deep sympathy in her green eyes. It seemed she was waiting for a cue to speak because she finally said, "I understand, Jeremiah. I could tell by the way you spoke of him in your letters when I already knew what he had forced on you. You still regarded him with respect and love in your words. That was... that meant a lot to me."

Jeremiah wasn't sure how to feel about that. The bungalow had come into view. He tried to look at it through her eyes as if he had never seen it before.

It was remarkably well kept. Another bonus for the gardener, who would also be in charge of the upkeep of the little building.

"Here it is."

He heard Isabelle gasp and glanced at her to take in her expression. She looked amazed, her eyes wide, her jaw slightly slack. "This is beautiful," she said.

He swung his gaze over the bungalow, the attached arched bridge that went over the creek, and the rippling water that ran underneath, sparkling in the bright sun. The grass looked greener there than anywhere else. He didn't know how that would be possible, but it sure seemed so to him.

"If there's anything you need in here, you let me

know. It should be freshly cleaned and stocked. It's frequently used by guests and sometimes us when we want a night away from the action of life."

Isabelle was quiet, but she looked impressed. He had a good feeling. She was going to give him a chance to redeem himself from this. He could feel worse that her first day there had turned into such a mess.

"We didn't get to eat our dinner," Isabelle mentioned.

"You're right," he said, his heart sinking for a moment. "But..." He grinned. "I'll go right back up and get it while you explore the bungalow and see if you need anything. I'll also have your bags brought down to you."

14

Jeremiah knew as he walked to the house that he was going to get into an argument with his mother. There was no doubt about that. He had a few words to say to her. He had to be respectful, but how she could insist that Victoriana stayed when he had obviously already taken care of the situation was beyond him.

He intended to apologize further to Victoriana. She was an innocent bystander in this situation.

But for now, all he wanted to do was get the food he'd prepared for the woman he'd invited to his home and take it to her.

He passed through the front door and went through the foyer, his eyes roaming around the house, wondering where his mother and Victoriana were. The room he'd had prepared for Isabelle was on the second floor, across the way from his own. To get to her room, it was a right turn on the landing, and his room was to the left. There was a great space between the two rooms, a fact he'd done on purpose so she wouldn't feel in the slightest way uncomfortable. If she wanted to move closer to him, there was another room next to his, but it was considerably smaller than the one he'd prepared for her.

Now Victoriana would be in that room. That was probably where she and his mother were at that moment.

He discovered he was wrong when he went into the dining room to retrieve the food.

His mother was seated in her usual chair at the head of the table opposite his chair, where his father used to sit. She was immediately glaring at him.

"Here you are. That took you long enough."

Jeremiah snorted. "Don't be that way with me, Mother. You've done me wrong, and I don't appreciate it."

She huffed, tossing her head back and forth, her nose in the air. "Nonsense. You are my son, and I know what's best for you. You didn't have a woman and chose not to inform me that you were speaking to someone. I didn't do anything or say anything about it until the beginning of this month when I knew your time was running out. It certainly didn't seem like you were worried about it at all."

Jeremiah clenched his jaw, pulling out a chair about halfway down the table and sitting in it. He didn't want to be too close to his mother, but all the way on the other side of the table was too far.

He put both arms up on the table and leaned toward his mother. He jabbed one index finger on the surface in front of him to stress his points. "I'm an adult, Mother. I didn't act worried because I wasn't worried. Listen, I understand that you thought you were doing what was right. But you should have told me what you were doing. You should have asked me before you went and told a woman she could come here, and we would court and then marry in the next twenty-five days."

His mother seemed nonplussed by his scolding. "I was doing something about the situation while you seemingly were sitting on your hands."

"I wasn't sitting on my hands, Mother," Jeremiah burst out, his voice slightly raised. A feeling of remorse slid through him, and he pulled himself back, getting under control. He cleared his throat, glancing toward the door as if he expected Victoriana or Isabelle to be listening on the other side.

More Victoriana than Isabelle. He was sure she was still out at the bungalow.

Thinking about leaving her there to look around filled him with a warmth he knew he wasn't going to get from any other woman. He temporarily lost his feelings of spite and anger at his mother.

Those feelings were mixed as it was. What she was saying was true. She hadn't done what she did out of malice. She thought he was being lazy. Many mothers thought their children were lazy when they weren't. But she hadn't done it to be mean. She hadn't even acted out of selfishness.

How could he stay angry with her when her intentions were good?

But it left him with quite a quandary on his hands.

"I'm sure Victoriana is a very nice lady," he added, his tone notably less upset. He was glad to see his mother's eyes flicker to him and some of the tension release from her taut face. "But, Mother, I've already made my choice." He disliked the hint of desperation he could hear in his own voice. "I like Isabelle. We've been talking through letters for weeks. I'm the one who started the whole thing. She responded to me."

"But how did you even find her to write to her?"

Jeremiah hesitated. He didn't want to reveal anything to his mother that Isabelle wouldn't want to be public knowledge. Should he tell her about the circumstances behind Isabelle's decision to leave Berkenshire?

He decided she didn't need to know everything. But she deserved to know as much of the truth as he thought ethical to share.

"I put an ad in a matrimonial magazine," he stated bluntly. "I thought it was the only way to get a woman that would know what she was stepping into."

His mother blinked at him. When she spoke, it was with great surprise. "You told this young woman why you wanted her to come here to marry you?"

Jeremiah's mind immediately dissected that question. He winced and flattened his lips before saying, "Well, not really. I did tell her in a way why I wanted her to come here. But in my second letter, I told her why I was looking for a bride. There's a difference. I didn't ask Isabelle to come here because I had to get married. I asked her to come because I found her to be intriguing and the woman I wanted to court."

He didn't like the way his mother rolled her eyes.

"Please don't react like that, Mother. She already

means a lot to me. She's a friendly woman with a good head on her shoulders. She is easy on the eyes, and I think we would have a wonderful life together."

"You don't know her. You have to keep your options open."

Jeremiah sighed heavily, dropping his forehead into one hand. "Mother," he groaned. "I was without any woman six weeks ago, and now there are two here vying for my hand in marriage." He looked up at her. "I'm just telling you right now, Mother. I've already made my decision. The only reason why I will entertain the idea of having Victoriana here is that she is innocent in this, and I can't see just sending her off without a by-your-leave."

When his mother smiled, he felt a little sick to his stomach. She was acting like she had won something. This wasn't a game. It was his life.

"I'm only being polite. Let's get that straight right now." He jabbed the table with his finger again, making his point harder. "I am not going to marry the woman you chose. I will marry the woman I chose. That's Isabelle. You'll have to get used to that because that's the way it's going to be."

The woman just grinned at him. "Wait until you

get to know Vicky. She's the sweetest girl in the world and will treat you like a king."

Jeremiah couldn't help recoiling at that idea. His mother acted like a queen. If that's how royalty behaved, he wanted nothing to do with it. He enjoyed being a rancher and doing things with his hands. He didn't want to rule over anyone and didn't want a woman to dote on him.

"I'm not a king," he said. "I don't want to be treated that way. I don't want a woman licking my boots. I want my woman to be happy, free to live her life."

"You'll see which one is the right one for you before the end of the month," his mother replied with surprising grace, though he was sure she was thinking of Victoriana, not Isabelle.

15

Jeremiah's heart beat anxiously in his chest as he saddled the horse for Isabelle. They had gone on a ride every day since she arrived, which was four days ago. It was the day that signified three weeks left until he was to be married.

He led the two horses out of the stable and to where she was waiting for him. She'd put on riding trousers, and he was amazed by how attractive she looked in them. The first time he'd seen her in them, he'd asked her what they felt like to her.

"They must feel very different," he had remarked.

She'd just grinned. "Probably how you would feel wearing a dress."

They'd both laughed—him mostly because he couldn't imagine ever doing such a thing or what that would feel like.

"Here you go," he said, handing her the reins. "You can ride Rosie. She seems to like you the best."

She smiled warmly at him. "That must be why you keep saddling her for me."

"That's exactly why. It's good to match a horse with a rider, and you two have similar personalities."

She gasped and laughed. "Did you just compare me to a horse?"

"I didn't mean to. Not like that. Not if it offends you."

He stumbled over his words, which only seemed to amuse her more. Her giggles were endearing her to him more than she realized.

"It's okay. I know what you meant. And I do like this horse very much." She gave the animal a pat on the neck and a smile. Jeremiah liked the way her eyes sparkled when she turned them up to the large beast. "Give me a hand up, please."

Jeremiah did so willingly, delighted by the touch of her skin on his when he lifted her up. He rested a hand on her waist to steady her at one point, and it sent a sock down his arm.

He pulled up into his own saddle, settling in

comfortably and turning the horse toward the path out into the woods.

"So, what are we going to talk about on this trip?"

"You decide," she responded to his question.

He had been working himself up to talk about Victoriana's presence and was curious what Isabelle was thinking about it. He cleared his throat and hesitated before blurting out, "I'd like to talk to you about Vicky."

He was pleasantly surprised to see she didn't look perturbed at the notion of wanting to talk about the third person in their relationship. Or whatever Victoriana was. He wasn't sure she was anything at all. Nothing more than a boarder. Possibly a friend. What would Isabelle think of his personal inner description of the Vicky he'd come to know?

"What are your thoughts on her?" he asked casually.

Isabelle was quiet for a moment. He glanced at her, but she was looking ahead and didn't turn her head to him.

"I like her," she finally said, putting it simply.

Jeremiah was relieved to hear it. He nodded. "I'm glad," he said. "I like her, too." This time Isabelle did look at him. He urged his horse to move a little closer to her. He rode along, staring right into her eyes, resting the reins clutched in his hand on the saddle horn. "Not like... not like I like you." He hoped his words didn't sound too boyish. He grinned. "I like you a lot more. But I can't say that I don't consider Vicky a friend now. She's been kind to me. She doesn't seem to be doing anything for nefarious reasons if you will."

Isabelle's expression hadn't changed. When she nodded, Jeremiah felt slightly taken aback, even though she hadn't shown any signs of resentment toward Victoriana on any occasion that he'd seen yet. Not to her face and not behind the woman's back.

"I haven't had a problem with her at all," she said. "But she doesn't go out to the bungalow. When I've had dinner in the house with you and your mother and her, I don't feel the conversation has struggled. Do you?"

He shook his head. "Not at all. She's a knowledgeable, amiable woman."

"And very good-looking. She's very pretty, isn't she?"

He detected a hint of something in her voice then that wasn't there any other time. He looked at her. "She's very brunette," he said simply.

Isabelle blinked at him, a smile wavering on her lips. "I beg your pardon?" she asked.

He chuckled. "Her hair is very dark. Her eyes are very blue. Her lips are very red. It's like she was made from a perfect mold. I'm not sure I'd want to have something like that on my arm. I'd be afraid of looking horrid next to her. Old and fat and horrid."

This made Isabelle burst out laughing. "Old and fat and horrid at twenty-four," she exclaimed, still laughing between her words.

"Hey," he responded, trying to be serious, "I won't always be twenty-four. I've got a lot of years to become really old. Fat. And boring, too. Can't forget that."

"You'll never be any of those things, Jeremiah, and you know it."

"So you aren't upset that Vicky has stayed on?"

"No." He was relieved by her answer. "I think she's got a good reason for staying. I mean, you and I might not work out. Your mother knows that, too. If something happens before your last three weeks are up and the wedding doesn't take place the day before, then you can just grab her and run to the courthouse."

He knew she was joking, but she was probably

right about the reasoning both Victoriana and his mother had for keeping her at the ranch.

"Well, nothing is going to stop it if I can help it," he said outright. "I asked you to come here with the intention of courting and marrying you. I hope you still feel the same as you did four days ago. It hasn't really been that long, but I feel like you fit in well. My men are on your side."

Isabelle blinked at him, and he suddenly realized how that must have sounded to her.

"I haven't been gossiping about you two," he said quickly. "They just know what's going on and know that I've been writing to you. They know that I chose you. I don't think I have to tell you that none of them hold much of what my mother does in high regard. She likes to think she rules the ranch now that father has gone, but unfortunately, her power didn't grow. In fact, they respect her less because of her. She demands a lot and doesn't give much in return. She's not gracious."

Isabelle didn't say anything. He was aware that she desired to respect his mother as much as possible. She'd told him as much on several occasions over the last couple of days. She didn't come to Texas looking for an opponent in the mother of the man she was planning to marry.

"I guess you're just trying to tell me that I have nothing to worry about where Victoriana is concerned. Is that right?"

"That's right," he said. "I have no one in my past and no one now that is more important to me than you."

He hadn't realized the weight or the impact his words would have on her. Her eyes widened slightly, and her mouth opened just a bit in a soft gasp.

He could only give her a warm smile. He meant what he was saying. As lovely as Victoriana was, Isabelle had already captured his heart. He wasn't about to ask for it back. All he wanted was Isabelle's heart in return.

16

After their long ride that afternoon, Jeremiah joined his crew to help tear down and replace one wall of the over-sized storage shed by the barn. They were about to break for the day, as the sun was lowering in the sky, and they wouldn't be able to see in a few hours.

Jeremiah was seated on the stump of a felled tree, drinking water from his canteen and wiping his forehead with the bandana he'd kept tied around his hat. He was soaked through with sweat. The work had been hard, but they'd replaced the entire wall in four hours, which was excellent in Jeremiah's opinion.

Brock knelt near him with one knee on the ground, lifting his own canteen to his lips. "Glad we got that done. We need to use that building. We have too much overstock for the summer."

"Yeah, I'm hoping we don't have trouble with rot this year."

They were quiet for a moment, both of them looking at the wall, admiring their own work.

After the last of the crew had left the area, Brock got Jeremiah's attention by clearing his throat and turning to him with a serious expression. "Listen, I wanted to ask you about something."

Jeremiah raised his eyebrows to acknowledge he was listening.

"Isabelle was out in the garden the other day with Vince. She pulled her sleeves up and was getting her hands real dirty diggin' up plants. Have you noticed those bruises on her arms?"

Jeremiah frowned. "I... bruises?"

He felt sick. Did Brock think he was being rough with Isabelle?

"I... haven't seen anything like that on her. But I haven't seen her bare arms." He was slightly jealous that Brock had seen a part of her he hadn't seen. Even something as insignificant as her lower arms.

Brock was quiet for another moment, looking out over the pasture. Jeremiah's stomach turned over and over. Brock's eyes darted to his face as he lifted the canteen to his mouth.

"You think somebody was hurtin' her over there in Virginia?"

Jeremiah's sick feeling turned to anger. "That can be the only explanation. I don't like to think she was gettin' hurt, but, well, ya sure the bruises looked like that? Maybe she's just clumsy."

Brock shook his head immediately, not taking his eyes from Jeremiah's as he said, "No. Sister of mine, June. Me and my brother saw those marks on her. She ain't married to the fella, I'll just say that. Those were the same marks. No doubt about it."

Jeremiah didn't know how to feel about that. He was grateful Brock had noticed such a thing, worried that the other men might think differently if they saw those bruises, and he couldn't help wondering if he should ask Isabelle about them. It was her business. He had nothing to do with it. They would heal. She was safe.

Unfortunately, that didn't satisfy Jeremiah's heart. He wanted to know what she'd been through. He would keep her safe, of course, but how could he help her heal if he didn't know what she'd been through?

"Thanks for tellin' me about it."

Brock nodded. "What are ya gonna do?"

"I don't think there's anything I can do."

"Seems to me you might have saved her from something awful."

Jeremiah couldn't bear the thought of it. This wasn't likely to leave his mind anytime soon. He wanted an explanation, but could he really ask her about something so personal.

Feeling confused, Jeremiah pushed up to his feet and stretched his muscles.

"You gonna go see her?"

Jeremiah nodded, turning his eyes in the direction of the bungalow. "Yeah. I wonder what she's doing?"

Brock said nothing more. Jeremiah didn't think about the fact that he didn't say goodbye. He was nearly to the bungalow before he thought about it. He turned and looked behind him, but Brock had left and was nowhere to be seen.

Jeremiah kept going, stepping off the stone path into the grass and heading for the front walk that led to the front door. There was an arch at the beginning of the walk, but he bypassed it, going onto the lawn and passing the flower bushes in front of the house.

He stopped abruptly, looking into the room through the window.

Jeremiah was not prone to peeping. He would never have continued looking in the window if he'd seen anything inappropriate. But what he did see intrigued him, and he had to stop. He didn't feel he had a choice.

She was standing inside, facing away from him at an angle. She had done some exploring, he noticed. That could be the only reason she had found the easel and the painting supplies. He didn't even know those things were still in the bungalow. They'd belonged to his sister, who had lived to be twenty years old before a strange illness made her waste away in the short span of six months.

The fact that the painting supplies belonging to his sister had been pulled from the oblivion of storage didn't have the impact on him he thought it might have. He and his mother still missed Carol every day, though he couldn't remember the last time they'd mentioned her. She'd only used the bungalow for her painting and hadn't gone there when she became ill. After she passed, their father put away all her things and left them in the darkness, forgotten.

Isabelle was staring at the painting in front of her.

Jeremiah wondered if it was one of her own or if

she was looking at one of Carol's. She'd left several unfinished.

She held the color palette in her left hand and a paintbrush in her right. The brush was up in the air as if she was waiting to decide what to do next.

When Isabelle moved slightly to the right, he felt a jolt of recognition. It was a painting of his sister's. There wasn't much done to it, but the outline was very clearly the bungalow itself. The growth around it was nothing like it was now, as it had been six years or more since his sister painted it.

She was wearing a painter's smock with half-sleeves. In the middle of her forearm, Jeremiah could clearly see a faded purple ring. It had been some time since the bruise had been left on her arm. But it was definitely just what Brock had said. He could see it had to be so, even though he'd never seen anything like that before with his own eyes. If Brock said he knew what it was, Jeremiah trusted he knew what he was talking about.

Jeremiah's heart wrenched in his chest. He didn't need another reason to fall for the woman in his bungalow or another reason to marry her. Seeing the bruise with his own eyes made him sure he was making the right choice. She had fled from something harmful and dangerous into his safe and loving arms. He would keep her away from danger if it meant giving his own life.

He moved away from the window, his desire to speak to her stronger now.

Before he knocked on the door, he thought about what he would say if she opened the door still in the painter's smock, allowing him to, at some point, "spot" the bruise and ask her about it. He could do it casually or with concern. How would he handle it?

17

Isabelle gazed at the painting, wondering who had done it. Intrigued by its beauty, she pulled it and all the painting equipment from the small closet they had been piled in.

She wasn't an artist herself. At least, she'd never given it a try. No one in her family had painted, so she never gave it a thought.

Now, with a paintbrush in her hand and a palate in the other with fresh paint she'd squirted on it, she was ready to try her hand. But first, she wanted inspiration.

Hence the half-done outline in front of her. A smattering of color had been added. It was obviously not something someone planned to finish.

Her plan was to look upon this painting in the

afternoon light and switch to a fresh canvas to start her own.

The knock on the door and the door opening itself let her know it had to be Jeremiah. No one else would just walk in like that.

Still, the thought that Percy had followed her and walked into her new little home set her heart to pounding at least momentarily. Her eyes darted to the opening to the living room through an archway.

Jeremiah appeared with a sheepish look on his face.

"I am so sorry. I shouldn't have just walked in. I won't do that again. I just... I saw you with the painting things out and thought I better come in and talk to you about them. These things aren't mine, and well, I'm not sure if my mother wants this partic-ular painting finished."

Isabelle stepped back, away from the easel. "I wasn't going to paint on it," she swore, shaking her head. "I promise. I was just looking at it for inspira-tion. There are empty canvases. I was going to use one of them. I was only trying to pass the time, that's all."

She hurried to set the palette and paintbrush to the side, eager to take down the forbidden painting that must remain unfinished.

He stepped closer to her, holding out both hands. "You don't have to do that," he said. "You can paint on the empty canvases. I just think you better not finish this one. It's not mine. It and all the rest of this stuff belongs... belonged to my sister. My older sister by two years. She passed away at twenty from an illness, and her things were stored here at the bungalow my father had built for her. She liked to get away from it all. She was the painter in the family. I tried. I can't do anything realistically."

"I've never really thought about it," she said, keeping the paintbrush in her hand but setting the palette down. She removed the unfinished painting from the easel. Setting it aside, she dragged her eyes from it to get an empty one and set it up. "You don't mind if I use an empty one?"

Jeremiah looked thoughtful, moving his gaze from to the easel and back. "I don't think Mother will really mind. I don't see why she even needs to know."

Isabelle gave him a serious look. "Are you sure you want to keep another secret from her? The last one didn't turn out really well. I'd hate to upset her with another one. I don't want to disrespect her. There's no reason I have to do this. I was just passing the time."

She let go of the empty canvas and stood up, somewhat eager to put the paintbrush down. She was almost embarrassed that she hadn't thought before about the implication of her actions. This wasn't her home. Those weren't painting supplies belonging to a relative.

She was barely being courted Jeremiah at this point.

Isabelle set to moving the easel to the side, propping it against the wall beside the enormous fireplace, which would have seemed out of place in the bungalow if it wasn't the only one and was required to heat the entire home during the winter.

There was no need for a fire, though, as it was quite warm enough at that time of year.

The paintbrush, palette, and tubes of paint had all come from a trunk with a latch closure. She set everything together and set the small trunk underneath the easel in between the legs.

When she turned back, she stopped abruptly, her eyes on Jeremiah. He was watching her. It wasn't that he was watching her so closely. It was the look in his eyes. It made her heart melt in her chest. She would have done anything he asked at that moment.

He must have seen the look on her face because he stood up from the edge of the couch where he'd been perched. He held out his arms to her. "You're a sweet woman, Isabelle. I hope you know it's you I want and not Victoriana. It's you I will be waiting by the preacher for on the day we are to be wed. I'm not trying to push you. We won't do anything until you are ready."

Isabelle couldn't resist moving into his arms. His hug was warm and loving. She closed her eyes and reveled in the sensation of having him so close to her.

She wished she could tell him they could get married the next day. But she needed a little more time. She didn't have the words to explain it to him either. She was just glad he was so understanding.

They parted with him still holding his arms up and letting her leave him slowly.

As he did so, his eyes slid down to her arms.

Tingles ran over her from head to toe when she saw his eyes light up on the ring of bruise around her forearm. She yanked away and pulled the half sleeve down to cover it, but it was too late.

Shame filled her. She sank to the couch, turning away from him at an angle. What would he think of her? What kind of woman would he think she was, coming to him with strange bruises that really could only be one thing?

She'd almost forgotten about those bruises. She didn't even see them anymore. They didn't hurt.

She felt him sit on the couch behind her.

"Listen," he said softly, catching her attention right away, "if you don't want to tell me how you got those bruises, it's all right with me. But I want you to know I'm not going to judge you for anything. You obviously didn't get them yourself. And from what I've seen of you so far, you aren't the type of woman to be involved with men who would treat you that way. So my thought is that you are running from a man who tried to control you. Probably a man with power who might eventually get the upper hand and have his way whether you like it or not."

Isabelle was amazed at his on-target intuition. She turned to him with wide eyes. He gave her a knowing look.

"I'm right, aren't I?"

She blinked at him, almost unable to speak.

"Y... yes. How... how did you do that? How did you guess so accurately and so quickly?"

He shook his head. "The process of elimination. You weren't a woman of the night, I know. I can tell by your demeanor. Your letters didn't indicate you were in fear for your life from someone in your family. You lived alone, after all. It had to be a man trying to intimidate you."

She stared at him for a few more moments. "Well, I am impressed."

He just grinned. "What do you think of having another dinner night tonight? Just you and me. I'll tell Vicky we're having dinner out here."

Isabelle nearly lost her breath. "You want to have a dinner night with Vicky here too?"

She almost laughed at the expression that came to his face. It was almost one of horror. "What? No. That's not what I... no..." He started laughing. "You and me, Isabelle. I'll tell Vicky so she doesn't worry and come find us."

"But your mother won't do that?"

He twisted up his face, and she knew his answer before he said it. "No, of course not. She wouldn't worry even if she noticed we didn't show up for dinner. She doesn't hate you, Isabelle. She's just keeping Vicky around in case you back out. She doesn't want to lose the ranch to Uncle Daniel any more than I do."

Isabelle thought that did make a lot of sense. "But won't Vicky be hurt?"

Jeremiah shrugged. "I guess not. She knows how the deal is going down and hasn't shown anything but friendship to both you and me. I don't know what's on her mind. I just know she isn't causing any trouble."

"I hope that continues," Isabelle murmured.

"Me, too."

18

———

Isabelle rested her head back in the folding chair, letting the sun's rays heat up the skin on her face. She reached up with one hand and adjusted the short cloth she'd put over her eyes so it wouldn't be too bright for her.

It was a calm, cool morning. The sun had yet to dry up the new morning dew. Isabelle had made a cup of coffee and was sitting on the lawn furniture, her cup next to her as she relaxed.

It had been ten days since her arrival. She had gotten permission from Clarice to use the paints and had set them up in the backyard behind the bungalow. The scenery was perfect there, and the trees overhead gave her plenty of shade.

She'd chosen the front yard that morning,

though, as the sun hit it first, and when the first light sparkled off the flowing water, it reflected the colors of the rainbow in the air. She loved it.

"Isabelle?"

She jumped a little, but Victoriana's voice was soft, so it wasn't too startling. She snatched the cloth off her face and pulled her head down to look through squinted eyes at Victoriana's smiling face. Her eyes reflected concern.

"I hope I didn't scare you too badly. I would have huffed and puffed and stomped over here, but I couldn't bring myself to do that and didn't know I would be catching you in a quiet time like this."

Isabelle had a feeling the woman would continue apologizing if she didn't stop her.

"It's all right, Vicky. Please, take a seat. Are you out for a morning stroll?"

Victoriana sat in the chair on the other side of the round iron table, setting her own coffee cup and saucer down as she did so. "I wasn't really, no. Breakfast isn't for an hour, and I thought I'd come out and have a little time to talk to you if you aren't busy."

Isabelle found herself to be a bit suspicious of the woman. What reason could she have to come to the bungalow for a special talk with Isabelle? Was she planning to threaten her? Or did she want to be friends?

Isabelle hoped it was the latter. She didn't like confrontation and would rather be on someone's good side if she had a choice. Pushing into a position where she was sitting up more in the long chair that let her stretch her legs out, she tried to calm her tingling nerves.

"What is it you wanted to talk about?" she asked, masking her nervousness the best she could.

Victoriana let her eyes wander over the beautiful scenery around her. "Oh, I was just thinking how we're both in quite the predicament. You, coming all the way from Virginia, me, here at the behest of my father." She glanced sideways at Isabelle. "I wonder, has Jeremiah said anything about my story?"

The fact that Victoriana was asking the question clued Isabelle into the fact that Jeremiah was seeing Victoriana when she wasn't around. Her stomach turned into a knot of jealousy, and she hated the feeling.

She forced friendliness into her voice.

"No," she replied, trying not to sound cold. "He hasn't said a word."

Apparently, she didn't hide how she was feeling as well as she'd liked.

Victoriana turned abruptly so that she was facing Isabelle. Her eyes were imploring. She stretched her hands out on the table between them. Her demeanor forced Isabelle to react, gazing directly at the woman.

"I want you to know that interfering in your… relationship was not my intention when I came here. I was under the impression Jeremiah didn't have anyone. We have met in passing, but I don't think he remembers. I barely do myself, as I was not expecting to be thinking of marriage with him."

The words made Isabelle's stomach turn over twice as violently.

"I am here because my father is anxious for me to marry, and Jeremiah seemed like a decent man when I agreed to it. I hadn't heard of any scandals surrounding him and only heard good things. But I want you to know, Isabelle, I am not in love with Jeremiah. In fact, I have no love for him at all. Not that kind." She smiled. "I could make myself if I wanted to. But when I saw the two of you that first night…" She shook her head, her smile disappearing from her face as quickly as it had come. "You two looked enamored with each other. To think that you had just arrived in Texas, I was very surprised to hear that."

Isabelle liked the way the conversation—if one could call it that when only one person had said anything so far—was going. She felt her body relaxing the more the woman spoke. The happiness invaded the negative feelings, pushing through until they were gone.

"I don't want to stand in your way. And I'm not staying here in the hopes that you will leave or he will ask you to." She stretched out one arm so her hand was closer to Isabelle. In response, Isabelle put her hand over Victoriana's. "I'm only here because my father will be furious when I go home, and I don't want to be there to announce that. I'm not trying to take advantage of the ranch or the kindness of Jeremiah and his mother."

Isabelle started at the words "kindness" and "his mother" in the same sentence. She stared at Victoriana.

"You really get along well with Clarice, don't you?"

Victoriana nodded, a look of innocence on her face. "You should have seen her after she discovered what Jeremiah did, bringing you here without telling her. She was a lot less angry than you might think. She was upset because she thought my father and I would be angry at her. She was hurt that Jeremiah didn't tell her what he was doing. I don't think she should have brought me here without telling him either."

Isabelle shook her head. "It seems like you're the one getting the short end of the stick, though. I'm sorry about that."

"It's the way of life," Victoriana responded, shrugging her shoulders. "I'll find the man I want to marry in my own time. My father may be displeased, but I cannot push myself on a man who has already given his heart to someone else."

These were the words Isabelle wanted to hear. She was glad Victoriana seemed to be turning out more friend than foe. She preferred things that way.

"Would you like some more coffee?" she offered, pushing off the chair. "Mine has gotten cold."

Victoriana looked down into her cup, also getting to her feet. "I think I do, yes. I don't suppose you have any sugar here?"

"Yes, they stocked the spices and sugar for me when I first arrived."

"This is a pretty little place to live." Victoriana ran her eyes over the top of the bungalow, taking in the whole little house. "I bet you'll be sad to leave when you marry Jeremiah and move into the big ranch house. I can't believe Clarice didn't open one of the other guest rooms for you. There are plenty."

"Perhaps it was meant to be," Isabelle answered, holding the door open for her new friend to come inside. "I'll be coming back frequently... whenever he starts getting under my skin."

Both women laughed.

19

Jeremiah strolled down the path, seeing the bungalow ahead of him. He'd noticed over the past few days that Victoriana and Isabelle appeared to have made friends. He didn't know how he felt about that. At first, he had the stomach-churning thought they might gang up on him and make his life miserable, both competing for his affections to see who would win. A little friendly rivalry, maybe.

But it hadn't worked out that way. Isabelle felt free to give him hugs and touch him randomly on his arms and shoulders when she was talking, and Victoriana did the opposite. She stood slightly away from them when the three were together but always had a friendly smile on her face.

It came as a tremendous relief to him.

His curiosity drove him to the bungalow that day. He hadn't seen Isabelle or Victoriana that morning. It seemed natural to wonder if they'd had breakfast together.

Therefore, he wasn't very surprised when he saw Victoriana coming toward him on the path when he moved around a curve.

She smiled brightly at him.

"Good morning," she said, her voice high and happy.

"Good morning. How is Isabelle?"

"She's feeling good. I was out on a stroll and stopped by. I'm sure she will be happy to see you. She's almost finished with that painting. I think it will be done by your wedding day. It's getting so close, isn't it?"

Jeremiah had to laugh inside. It appeared the woman was more excited about his wedding than he was. And she wasn't even his prospective bride.

He glanced at the bungalow ahead and gave her a sneaky look. "So... what does it look like? Is it the bungalow? Is it me? It's me, isn't it? I just know it's me."

She laughed, sending a thrill through him. He

had to chuckle more at her response than his own joke.

"I'm not telling," she said, giggling out the words. "You'll like it, I promise. You go on now. I'm sure she will be happy to see you."

"Where are you going today?" he asked out of curiosity.

"I'm heading into town with your mother. I believe she wants to pick up some ingredients for a special dinner. Byyyyyeee..." She sang out the last word as she slipped past him and continued hurrying up the trail.

He watched after her for just a moment before turning back to the bungalow and going on his way.

Isabelle was looking particularly bright and pretty that morning. She was sitting on the porch with a large sketchpad on her lap and a charcoal stick in her hand. He'd noticed that since she started taking up painting and sketching, her right hand was always dirty or black with charcoal dust.

He was amused to see she was wearing a glove this time. She saw him coming and set her pad aside, a big smile on her face. She jumped up and came toward him.

"I was wondering when you were going to come

to find me," she called out before he got to her. "Do you want to have lunch with me?"

"I think that's a wonderful idea," he replied, quickening his steps as his heart did the same. "Did you have breakfast?"

"Yes, but that was hours ago. I'm famished now."

She excitedly stepped down to the walk and waited for him there, bouncing on her toes.

Jeremiah's eyes flickered to the sketchpad, wondering if she would let him see what she'd been drawing. She must have seen where his gaze was going because she glanced over her shoulder.

"You want to see what I've been sketching?" she asked, grinning wide. She spun around and ran to the table, snatched up the pad, and brought it over to him, holding it out eagerly. "What do you think? Honest opinion now. I never thought much about my artistic skills, but I think being in such a lovely place has brought it out in me."

She pressed the pad into his hands, and Jeremiah began to flip through it. Each sketch was better than the last.

He let out a low whistle, flipping through it. There were a few sketches of him and a few of Victoriana, some of the bungalow and some of the creek nearby, but none of his mother. He wouldn't ask why.

He didn't have to. Although she and Victoriana had made friends, Isabelle still seemed sore over the slight his mother had done to her.

"You are talented," he said. "You might end up becoming a famous artist."

Isabelle rolled her eyes. "Well, I don't know about that," she replied, "but I am having fun. And I do have my special project, too, don't I? You are going to love it, I'm sure of it."

"That's what Victoriana says, too. I guess we'll see. It feels like I'm never going to get a chance to get a look at it. You two keep teasing me about it."

"I guess we really shouldn't," Isabelle said in a thoughtful tone. "What if you hate it? What if you think it looks like a child did it? I don't think I want your honest opinion, after all. Just say you love it and tolerate it being over the mantle the rest of your life, all right?"

He laughed. "I guess I can tolerate that." He handed the sketch pad back to her. "These are good, though. They really are. You should definitely keep doing that. Build up your skill. You never know where it might take you."

She raised her eyebrows. "Do you know people in the industry?"

"The art industry?" Jeremiah searched his mind

as quickly as he could but shook his head at her. "Not me, no. My mother might."

He almost choked on laughter when a look of scorn appeared on Isabelle's face for just a moment.

"I don't think I'll ask her for advice or help," she said.

Jeremiah shook his head. "You and my mother will have to call a truce eventually, you know. I see you and Vicky are getting along now. How did that happen?"

If he'd been asked, Jeremiah would have said he saw a look of relief on Isabelle's face when the subject matter changed.

"She came here to the bungalow a few days ago to talk to me over breakfast. I didn't know her story. She is being forced to be here, you know. By her father."

Jeremiah nodded. He'd talked to Victoriana one on one several times, just telling her he welcomed her to stay as a friend, but there wouldn't be anything more between them. She seemed quite conciliatory and was willing to go along with his plan to ultimately keep his mother from complaining until the day of the wedding arrived, and Isabelle was still the woman walking down the aisle on his arm.

Jeremiah didn't care that she'd answered his ad any more than she cared that he'd placed it. His reasons were solid, and hers seemed the same to him.

"She is a very understanding woman," he answered her while nodding. "I've spoken to her alone a few times, and she doesn't want to be my wife." He chuckled, noticing when Isabelle smirked. "Which, I'm sure you know, is fine with me. I can't have two wives, can I?"

"I suppose you could if you wanted two," Isabelle replied, "but those two wouldn't be myself or Victoriana. Neither of us would stoop to something like that."

He nodded. "Nor would I. So all I can do is thank her for not wanting to interfere with us."

"Wait here. Let me take this inside. We can go to town if you want, or you can make something here. It's up to you."

"I'm not in the cooking mood," he said casually, pondering it for a moment. He raised his eyebrows, gazing at her. "Are you?"

"No. I want someone to cook for me. Let's go to town."

He laughed. "All right, let's do that."

20

With just one week left until they were to get married, Isabelle was feeling more secure than ever. She had three weeks of time in Texas and was more and more comfortable calling it her home. She couldn't imagine going back to Virginia now, though she did miss Margie quite a lot. Her letters to her friend were filled with happy words and interesting stories.

She told Margie what had happened with Victoriana as soon as it happened, in plain words, and was on the receiving end of some heartfelt encouragement from the friend she'd left behind.

Since Victoriana's admission that she had no feelings for Jeremiah other than friendship, Isabelle had absolutely no intention of ever returning to Berkenshire.

The weekend would be filled with festival fun. The town had come together to throw the big party, as they did every year, Isabelle came to find out. She waited anxiously outside the bungalow, on the arched bridge, looking down at the rippling water. Jeremiah would come to get her when he was ready. He would be her escort, and they would be meeting Victoriana there.

Isabelle grinned, her eyes following the moving water, remembering what a big deal Victoriana had made out of meeting her there instead of going with them in the same buggy. She'd insisted—and would not take no for an answer—stating very firmly that she was not going to give the impression that she was vying for Jeremiah's hand or posed any threat to Isabelle. She also believed firmly that despite the constant prodding of Clarice, she could convince everyone that she was only there as a visitor, not as a possible bride for Jeremiah.

When she saw Jeremiah coming down the path toward her, a big smile on his face, her heart did a little flip in her chest. She enjoyed the butterflies that burst to life in her stomach. She'd never felt so content in her life.

"There she is," Jeremiah said as he got closer as if he'd been looking high and low for her. She was already smiling but couldn't help stretching it a little wider.

"Here I am. I'm so looking forward to having fun with you at this festival. I'll be very honest with you. I didn't attend many of the parties put on by the Berkenshire council. They always seemed so boring to me."

Jeremiah's eyebrows shot up. "How can a party be boring?"

Isabelle laughed, remembering the townsfolk's attempts to put on something fun for the community. "Bland food, boring music, badly written and acted plays... no games. No prizes."

As she spoke, Jeremiah's face went blank until he was just staring at her, blinking. "You're right," he said plainly. "That doesn't sound like much fun." His teeth flashed when he suddenly smiled. "But you're going to have fun with me today. Let's go. Vicky and Mother are already on their way."

He stretched out his hand, and she took it, enjoying the tingling sensation that ran up her arm when their skin touched. He pulled her closer, making her heart beat hard.

"Can I ask you something?" she asked as they

went back toward the stable where the buggy was waiting.

He gave her a curious look. "Certainly. Tell me what you're thinking."

Isabelle gazed into the distance in front of them, not really focusing on the buggy even though she was heading toward it. "I was thinking this morning about my aunt and uncle and how they stepped up and raised me when I lost my parents. I was young." She tilted her head, giving him a soft look. "I wonder how different it is for you, being an adult and losing a parent. You seem to be handling it well. I know it must hurt to have him gone from your life."

Jeremiah appeared to be thinking about it. He gave her a nod and helped her up into the buggy. She settled in as he went around and got up in the driver's seat. He slapped the reins to pull the horses to the left toward the pathway to the main road.

"I loved my pa." She heard the melancholy in his voice. "And the stipulation to marry by three months came as a real surprise. I don't want you to think I'm unhappy with him for it. I was taken aback at first. Of course I was. I was a little angry."

The buggy jostled Isabelle to the side, and she bumped into him. He smiled at her and purposefully bumped her back.

His lips settled when he continued, "What I didn't know was that Mother had told him Betty and I at the shop in town were getting close. He thought I had a sweetheart. He just wanted to make sure I didn't drag my feet, I guess. I wish he'd talked to me about it. I guess he just never got around to it."

Isabelle let a moment linger before she said quietly, "What would you have done if he told you he was going to do that?"

Jeremiah sighed. He didn't answer at first. She knew he'd heard the question. He was just thinking about it.

"I really don't know. I wouldn't have known that Mother had lied to him about Betty and me. I would have told him he was out of his mind and not to do something like that to me. I didn't want to get married. The thought was never even on my mind."

"But it's not like that now, is it?" she asked playfully.

He grinned at her, snorting softly through his nose. "You know it isn't. I'm fully aware that we will be married in less than ten days. And we're going to have a wonderful life together. You just wait and see."

Isabelle loved the sound of that. She moved closer to him so their arms brushed against each other. Her heart slammed in her chest when he wrapped his arm around her and squeezed.

THE FESTIVAL WAS in full swing when they got there. Jeremiah found an empty slot in the dirt lot to leave the buggy.

Isabelle was immediately overcome with excitement. Walking into the crowd that filled the main street and square made her feel like a small girl enjoying fun for the first time. It felt like years since the last time she was in a crowd of happy people having a good time. She turned in a half-circle, taking it all in. There were games, cotton candy stands, popcorn stands, and sack races. She didn't know there were that many children in Low Branch.

"This is delightful," she gushed, sliding her hand around his arm. She pushed her shoulders against him, giggling like the schoolgirl she felt inside, eager to come out and play some games.

"I'm glad you like it," he responded, patting the hand she'd put around his arm. "You look like you've never been to one of these before."

"Well, considering I've only been here a few weeks, I can safely say you'd be right about that."

For the next several hours, Isabelle and Jeremiah wandered around, playing games and eating popcorn with caramel on top. Isabelle met several people who clued her in to the kind of man Alexander Connelly had been. From what they said, he was kind and generous, intelligent to a fault, and full of good advice for younger people coming up in business or young men with personal problems.

By the time the noon hour came around, and the two were ready to eat, Isabelle found herself wishing she'd met the man before he'd passed. He seemed to be quite intriguing.

Isabelle's stomach grumbled. She set her hand on it, smiling up at Jeremiah, who chuckled. "Let's find Vicky and see if she wants to get something to eat at the restaurant."

Jeremiah nodded. "She's got to be hungry after walking around with my mother all day long."

"She might need a strong drink instead of food," Isabelle quipped.

Jeremiah laughed appreciatively while Isabelle tried not to feel bad about making a joke at Clarice's expense.

She spotted Vicky near the barber shop where they had a balloon popping contest going on.

Her eyes didn't stop focusing when she saw the

young woman, though. There was a man behind her. A man whose shoulders hunched over, his hat pulled down as if he was trying to hide.

But she knew who he was.

Isabelle knew exactly who he was.

21

When Isabelle let out a sudden gasp and practically collapsed next to him, Jeremiah was taken by surprise. He managed to grab her before her knees went completely out. She was suddenly white as a ghost. She looked up at him with frightened eyes.

"I... I don't feel so good. We have to go. Please. I need to go. Can we go home?"

"Of course," he exclaimed. Despite how it might look, he put his arm under her knees and swept her off her feet, cradling her against him. He hurried to the buggy, which was fortunately not far from where they were. He saw Vicky turn and look at them as he hurried away from the barber shop where she'd been playing the balloon game.

A look of shock came over her face, and her steps turned toward them. She was quickly beside them, giving Isabelle a look of concern.

"Oh my," she exclaimed. "What's happened? Is she okay? Is it something you ate? What did you eat, Isabelle?"

Jeremiah looked down to see Isabelle looking around Vicky to the barber shop again. His eyes darted in that direction as well to see what she was looking at. He didn't see anything but a game of balloon darts going on.

"It's not something I ate, Vicky," Isabelle responded breathlessly.

"She was feeling faint," Jeremiah put in. He lifted her up, and she climbed into the buggy. He turned his gaze to Vicky. "Probably too much sun. It's not like Virginia here. Different climate."

"That's not it," Isabelle said softly, holding onto the railing beside her and leaning toward the two of them. Jeremiah gave her his full attention, aware that Vicky was doing the same thing right next to him.

"What is it then?" Vicky asked, her voice equally low.

Isabelle hesitated, looking up and behind them. Jeremiah had a strong feeling she was looking toward the barber shop again. He wondered who she was looking at. He'd seen several strangers, but that didn't surprise him. Relatives and people who used to live in Low Branch often came back for the weekend festival for various reasons.

He resisted the urge to look back. She was about to tell them. He wanted to hear every word and not be distracted looking for a stranger.

"I left Virginia... well, one of the reasons I left was because a certain man was pursuing me. He had some influence in Berkenshire—at least his father did, as he is the mayor there. He's a good man, the mayor. His son is not of the same mold."

"He's here?" Jeremiah asked, guessing at what she was going to say next. Her eyes darted to his face, a frightened look permeating her fine features.

"Yes," she replied, her voice quivering. "I saw him by the barbershop. Near you, Vicky. That's when I almost collapsed. I can't believe he is here. Why would he come all this way for me?"

"How could he possibly have afforded to do such a thing?" Vicky asked. "Did his father also want the two of you to marry?"

Isabelle shook her head. "He was unaware of my feelings. He thought the union was desired by us both. I would have talked to him about it, but, well, talking to him wouldn't have stopped Percy."

"So this Percy is here, is he?" Jeremiah asked. "What does he look like?"

Jeremiah's chest tightened to a painful point, thinking about a man coming from Virginia to steal his woman away. He wasn't going to let that happen. He would stop it no matter what he had to do.

Isabelle's eyes were filled with tears as she looked over their heads and then back to them, first him, then Vicky, then back. Her eyes wouldn't stay in one place for longer than a second. His heart ached for her. She was truly frightened. He'd never expected to see her look that way. She was so outgoing and friendly and fun. This Percy must have truly bothered Isabelle.

And coming across half the country told him the man was more than enamored with Isabelle. He likely thought of her as his property that had gotten away. A mayor's son. Entitled to whomever he wanted to marry.

She dropped her eyes to his face once more. "Can you please just take me home? I don't want to be here anymore. I don't know if he's seen me yet or found out where I live yet. I don't even know how he could possibly have found out where I moved to."

"Have you been writing to anyone?"

Vicky asked the question as she pulled herself

into the back seat of the buggy. She scooted to the middle of the seat and leaned forward so she could see between Isabelle and Jeremiah, who went around to get up into the seat next to Isabelle.

Isabelle turned her back to the commotion and faced him as he pulled himself up. He kept his eyes on her settling down and taking the reins in his hands.

"I have been writing to my friend Margie," she answered, "but I don't believe she would tell him anything. The only way he would have gotten that from her is if he hurt her."

Isabelle's eyes opened wide. Jeremiah clenched his jaw momentarily. "Don't think about that, Isabelle," he said quickly. "I'm sure your friend is fine."

When she gave him a confused look, he knew why. How could he possibly know such a thing? Even he had to admit the statement had absolutely no weight to it.

"Do you want to stop at the postmaster and send a letter out to her?" he asked, hoping his suggestion would redeem him.

She nodded, sniffing, tears suddenly in her eyes.

"You don't want to do that," Vicky said, getting their shocked attention. Jeremiah was about to scold her for her opinion when she continued, "You need to go home. I'll send the message. Does the Postmaster have the address?"

Isabelle shook her head.

Jeremiah watched as the women went through their bags for something they could use for writing down the address for Vicky. He turned the horses gently in the right direction, stopping in front of the building so Vicky could get out. She gave Isabelle a hug around the shoulders from behind and promised to make sure it was all taken care of correctly.

"I'll bring you back any message I might receive in return."

"I hope she's all right," Isabelle murmured tearfully. Jeremiah put his arm around her shoulders.

"We'll pray she is," he said as quietly, getting them back on the road.

She was quiet as a church mouse all the way back to the ranch. Jeremiah's emotions were so mixed he barely knew what he was feeling.

He was completely invested in making sure Isabelle said "I do" in nine days. Everyone was expecting it, even his own mother. Clarice hadn't really warmed up to Isabelle and still told him whenever she had a chance that Victoriana was a much more suitable match, but he knew why she was saying those things.

Someone's last name and status in society meant nothing to Jeremiah. He was concerned only with what was on the inside. He didn't want a flashy woman of society that everyone knew and had feelings about. Not that he cared about that either.

Stability was what he was looking for. A companion who would make him smile and laugh, who would cook with him and sing with him, a woman who could paint him a beautiful picture with a brush and some paints.

His thoughts made him laugh.

Suddenly he had a list when a few short months ago, marriage was the furthest thing from his mind.

Isabelle had changed all that.

22

Jeremiah waited by the door of the breakfast nook, staring out past the veranda to the arched bridge over the creek. He didn't see any movement. He'd been gazing out in that direction for the last ten minutes to see her when she crossed over the bridge to get to the path. They'd decided to spend the rest of the day relaxing. It was Sunday, and the festival was starting up early as usual, but there would be a break in most of the festivities when nearly the entire population went to church.

Jeremiah attended with his mother and the other two ladies typically.

That day, their plan was to keep an eye out for

Percy. When she saw him, Isabelle would let him know, and she would go home after pointing him out. Jeremiah would then have a stern talk with the man, demand to know what he was doing chasing Isabelle down, and, as the intended husband, ask him politely to get out of town and go back to Virginia.

But Isabelle hadn't crossed the bridge. She was still in her house. Or she had left early and gone where? Where would she have gone?

Jeremiah refused to entertain the idea that Isabelle had gone to find Percy herself. She had been afraid of him. There was no mistaking that. She was scared to death. If she was in love with the man or had any reason to want to be reunited with him, Jeremiah felt sure he would have seen it somehow.

He sensed someone coming up behind him and turned his head to see it was Vicky. Her eyes were focused out the window toward the bungalow as well.

"Where is she?" she murmured. "I'm famished and simply must get something in my stomach before we go today. I'm so nervous for her."

She finally moved her gaze to him. He said nothing.

She looked perplexed, her eyes darting back to the pathway.

"Where... where is she, Jeremiah? You don't think... she didn't..."

Jeremiah shook his head. "No. I don't think she went looking for him. She wouldn't do that. Would she? No. She wouldn't." He battled with himself to answer the question the best he could.

"Neither of us really know her that well, though, do we?" Vicky queried.

"We can't think like this. There's another explanation. Come on."

With that, Jeremiah stepped determinedly toward the double glass doors. He went through and down the stone steps to the lawn below. She was on his heels a few minutes later, realizing what he was doing.

"You're going to check on her? Do you think she'll be all right with that?"

Jeremiah pulled his eyebrows together, giving her a strange look. "You've shown up without letting her know in the morning before, haven't you? Did she resent it then?"

Vicky shook her head. "No, but you know this situation is different. She might feel like you're checking to make sure she is still here."

Jeremiah huffed. He wouldn't let his temper get away from him. "I am checking to make sure she's still here. And if she is, I'm checking to make sure she's all right."

Vicky smiled. "I'm just making sure you're sure what you're doing."

"I'm sure."

He trotted eagerly over the lawn to the pathway and then the arched bridge.

The bungalow was quiet. If she was awake, Isabelle was motionless. He could feel the calm in the air. It hadn't been disturbed by movement yet.

"Isabelle?" he asked, knocking with his knuckles as he pushed open the bungalow door.

"Jeremiah..." He heard her voice from the other room and instantly thought she sounded very sick. He practically ran through the small building to the back room to see Isabelle laid out on the bed, her hair plastered to her head and the pillow soaked through.

"What in heaven's name?..." He rushed over to her bed, placing his hand on her forehead once he was there. She was burning up. Worry sliced into him, making his body tense. He looked over his shoulder.

"I... I..." Isabelle's voice trembled as she tried to

speak. "I can't keep anything... down... I don't know... what's wrong..."

She writhed in pain. Her face stretched with agony. He could see it in her eyes when she looked at him.

"When did this start?" he asked, gesturing to Victoriana to bring him a cloth from the kitchen. "Put some water on it from the pump," he instructed before turning back to Isabelle. "My poor girl. You could only have been poisoned."

"But why..." she murmured. "The only... only person who could have done this is... is... Percy. But he's not clever enough to figure something like this out. I just don't think he is."

"Well, even if he was," Vicky said, coming back with the cloth, "how would he have gotten the poison to you? What have you eaten or drank since we saw you yesterday?"

Jeremiah looked to Isabelle for her answer, but she looked perplexed and was shaking her head ever so slightly.

"I just... I just don't know... who would do this other than Percy. But you're right. How could he have made sure I got the poison at all?"

"Maybe he took a chance that you would come in contact with it."

"But other people would be sick, too, wouldn't they?" Jeremiah asked. "I'm sorry to poke holes in that, but if Percy poisoned you, he's more clever than I am."

"It could only have been him. The only other person who doesn't like me... well..." She didn't continue. The thought that Clarice might be the one doing the poisoning didn't sit well with Jeremiah either. His mother wasn't the type to take things that far.

Would she?

He would have to get his answer somehow. He'd found in the past it was best to just ask her outright and see how she answered.

"Help me back to bed," she begged him. His heart ached for her. He gathered her in his arms, planting soft kisses on her cheeks and forehead. He couldn't help it.

If his mother was responsible for Isabelle's pain, he would have a few choice words to say to her. He was hoping beyond hope she wasn't the one who had told Percy where to find Isabelle. How would she know what kind of trouble that might get Isabelle in? Surely his mother wouldn't put the woman he loved in a position to lose her life to a crazy lunatic.

Would Clarice put any woman in jeopardy of losing her life to a violently obsessed man?

He swooped her up into his arms and carried her from the floor in front of the couch to the bedroom in the back. He laid her on the bed and stepped back to examine her. She looked normal other than the obvious pain in her eyes and the way she flexed her hands.

They had come quickly to the decision that someone had poisoned her. But maybe this was caused by something else. Either way, the doctor needed to be called for, and that's what he planned to do right then.

"I'm going to get the doc," he said, knowing his voice sounded strained. He was a little surprised how much seeing her like this made him feel pain for her. She'd taken his heart.

Jeremiah leaned over and wrapped his arms around her shoulders, pulling her into a hug. She groaned, but he knew it wasn't because of what he was doing. He plastered kisses on her face, and for the first time, the last one was on her lips. She responded in kind, and the kiss lasted until he couldn't breathe anymore. He pulled away and pressed his forehead against hers, despite the fact it was covered in sweat.

He didn't care. He loved her.

"I'm sorry this happened to you. I'm so sorry. I'm going to figure out who did this."

"Okay, Jeremiah," she responded in a breathless way. "Thank you."

He stood up, turning to her.

"You stay here with her," he instructed Vicky, who nodded as if he had the right to demand anything of her. He felt she wanted to stay and help out. He'd discovered she was very good at helping when she was needed, a trait that made him want to keep her at the ranch in some other kind of capacity. Not necessarily a maid. Perhaps an assistant of some kind.

He thought about these things to distract himself from hurting for Isabelle. She looked like she'd been up all night vomiting. From the smell in the bungalow, he was pretty certain that was an accurate assessment.

As he went out, he opened several windows wide. He left the door halfway cracked to let the interior air out.

He was halfway down the path and almost to the arched bridge when he realized what he'd done. In order to let the bungalow air out, he'd put the women in terrible danger. He rushed back to the bungalow, his eyes alert to every movement of the leaves and bushes around him. He saw no strange man lurking but wasn't going to take any chances. Vicky could go for the doctor. He would stay with Isabelle and keep her safe.

23

───────

Isabelle stared at Jeremiah, still feeling weak from whatever had made her ill.

The doctor had ruled out insect bites and everything except the ingestion of poison, which he insisted must have happened at the festival. He saw no other way it could have gotten into her. He had many long-named guesses for what she'd been poisoned with, but in the end, it took a full day of rest for her to feel normal again.

The main symptom left over from the poison was a feeling of being drained. At least, that was the way it was with her. That and a terrible headache.

Victoriana had been sitting with her all morning. Now Jeremiah had come to give her the worst news she could have heard.

He didn't look like he wanted to give her his news, so she was less angry with him than she was with the circumstances.

"I wish they would just come here and let you sign the papers," she whined, pushing out her lower lip. She saw the look of adoration on his face, and affection swept through her.

"You know they can't do that for me," he said softly, touching under her chin with two fingers. She loved how gentle he was with her. He made her feel so cared for.

"I'm just so… on edge. I know that was Percy I saw." Isabelle truly didn't care for how weak her voice sounded right then. She was sure. Wasn't she?

She thought back to when she'd seen the man behind Victoriana. He'd had his head down. He was wearing a long, tan trench coat with a lot of pockets.

She couldn't say she'd ever seen Percy in an outfit like that. It looked like he belonged in Texas.

Isabelle didn't know enough about Percy to be able to judge whether he was wise to Texas ways or not. He was a mayor's son, but Berkenshire wasn't New York City. His father didn't have a great deal of influence. He'd never meet the President. He was a small cog in a large machine.

Still, he could easily have traveled. Anytime in

his considerably more years than Isabelle's. He could have traveled abroad for all she knew.

Now, doubting that she actually saw Percy since he hadn't shown up at the bungalow, Isabelle just hoped she wasn't losing her mind. Jeremiah wouldn't want to marry a crazy woman. And she didn't want to be locked away for paranoid delusions.

"I'm going to have Brock check on you constantly," Jeremiah said, answering her question about whether he remembered she might be in danger.

Isabelle wondered if she should tell him she'd doubted the man she saw was actually Percy. She wanted to be taken seriously and didn't want to be left in a potentially dangerous position. But she also didn't want to look like she was scared of every strange man she saw. She didn't want to be the "boy who cried wolf" or girl, in her case.

She didn't voice her thoughts. He didn't seem overly concerned. Brock checking on her should be enough.

She nodded at him. "Thank you for that," she said. "I'm sure everything will be fine."

His eyebrows shot up, and he gazed at her. "You aren't afraid of Percy finding out where you are?"

Isabelle darted her eyes out the window. It was

all right with her if he knew she was uncomfortable. She just didn't want to tell him she doubted her very sanity.

Surely Percy hadn't damaged her so much that she would keep seeing him everywhere.

"I feel like I'll be safe as long as I don't venture off your land. If he finds me here while you're gone, I'll have my gun by my side."

Jeremiah gave her a doubtful look, and she knew why.

"You think you will be able to shoot him?" he asked skeptically.

"I will have to. If he gets aggressive."

"I just hope you'll have the presence of mind to shoot at least once in the air, maybe through a window if you're inside, so Brock will hear and come running. He won't come alone, I promise."

He tapped her on the nose and grinned, sending a sweep of affection through Isabelle.

"All the men on the property think you're a great lady. They say you will be a good wife to me and will have this place running smoothly as the mistress."

Isabelle tilted her head to the side, a pleasant feeling washing over her. "That is so nice to hear. You just hurry back. You'll only be gone for one day?"

"Just one day. I'm leaving in a few hours and will be gone overnight. I'll sign the papers in the morning and be back by four or five tomorrow afternoon."

"I understand not wanting to make that trip all at once. You would be exhausted, wouldn't you?"

He pulled her into a hug that allowed her to hear his heart beating in his chest.

"Yes. Too exhausted even to sign documents with a real signature of any kind."

She felt him chuckle, and she smiled wide, closing her eyes and resting her head against his chest. She felt so protected in his arms. So safe from anything harmful.

"When are you leaving?"

"In a few hours. I thought I'd come and say goodbye first. Give me time to get my things together."

"I'm going to miss you so much."

His face was bright with a smile when he pulled away from her.

"I'll miss you, too. I know it sounds silly for both of us to say that, but I'm very ready to be married to you, Isabelle. I'm a little surprised by how, I don't know, comfortable I feel about the whole situation.

My father..." He shook his head. "I guess he knew what he was doing."

"Maybe he got a sign he should do that before he passed," Isabelle suggested. "That would mean we are meant to be, wouldn't it?"

"Yes. And we are."

"Jeremiah."

Isabelle jumped when she heard Clarice shriek Jeremiah's name from the other side of the arched bridge.

He turned to her. Isabelle couldn't see his face, but she was willing to bet he was glaring at the woman.

"Mother. You nearly frightened us to death. What do you want?"

Isabelle pulled out of his arms, feeling cold when the breeze moved between them. She wanted to lean back into him, not allow him to let her go.

"It's time to pack and get things ready. No time for this. She will be fine. Come along."

Isabelle realized at that moment Jeremiah had to go with his mother to sign the legal documents. She instantly felt sorry for him.

Just to make a point, she pulled him to her and planted a long kiss on his lips, glad to see the stunned, outraged look on his mother's face and a sly look come to Jeremiah's.

24

Isabelle had dozed off on the outer deck on the creek side of the bungalow. She'd been resting with Victoriana hovering around the bungalow all day, slowly recovering from the poison that had mysteriously entered her body.

The doctor had recommended nothing but rest and something that made her have to use the outhouse more often than she would have liked as her body expelled the bad stuff.

But that horrific process seemed to have passed, and now she was feeling much better. The sun had helped, too, so she was basking in it, waiting for Jeremiah to return.

It had been an uneventful night. She hadn't

attended dinner at the main house. Victoriana had brought her something out of the kindness of her heart, and the two women sat to enjoy crackers and wine and talk about men and other intriguing topics.

She'd woken up that morning feeling nearly recovered with only the trips to the outhouse to complain about. She was grateful to be alive. That was what mattered. She had a future ahead of her, one that included Jeremiah. She wanted the chance to live a happy life with him, have his children, and help him around the ranch.

Behind her closed eyelids, Isabelle saw a vision of Jeremiah on the porch of the ranch house, standing with his mother. She was perplexed by his attitude. He was gesturing wildly at her, but she couldn't hear any of the words coming out of his mouth.

Off to the side of the porch, she saw Clarice and Percy, their heads tilted together, their hands up as they hid their words from the world. Their eyes looked evil.

In the next moment, the two were directly in front of her, their hands reaching out for her.

The thought that they were going for her

throat… they were going to kill her… flashed through her mind.

She gasped audibly and sat up, opening her eyes. She looked around her frantically.

There was no one around.

Her heart didn't accept that fact. It continued to pound as fear coursed through Isabelle's body. She could try to fool herself all she wanted. Percy was in Low Branch. She had seen him. It was him. She knew it was. It had to be. No one else made her feel that way, like he was looking into her soul whenever their eyes met. It made her feel slimy inside.

She tried to slow her breathing. There was no one around.

Isabelle consciously took a breath in and let it out slowly. She settled back in the chair, hoping Victoriana would come back soon. She was probably somewhere nearby. When she wasn't, Brock usually was. Isabelle wasn't sure how she felt about constantly having bodyguards know exactly where she was at all times.

Especially because they hadn't figured out how she'd been poisoned or if it was really Percy she'd seen.

Isabelle tried closing her eyes. After a few

attempts, she knew that was going to be impossible. She would have to find something else to do. Sleep was out of the question.

She grasped both arms of the chair she was seated in and pushed up.

She wasn't on her feet yet when she felt a hand wrap around one of her wrists. She looked back, her heart jumping in her chest. Her hand was yanked off the armrest, causing her to fall back, or her wrist would be twisted. She pushed her feet down hard and quick to pivot herself up. Her only intention was to get rid of Percy, who had grabbed her and was glaring at her with a look of hatred.

"What are you doing here?" she asked, trying hard to wrench her wrist from his tight grasp. "How did you find me? What do you want? Leave me alone."

"You are coming back to Virginia with me," Percy growled, his dark eyes narrow and menacing.

Shock covered Isabelle from head to toe.

"What are you talking about?" she asked, knowing it was nearly inaudible because she was finding it hard to breathe.

"You aren't wanted here. I know that man you think you're in love with is in love with you, but he isn't. You came over here because of a magazine. He loves that dark-haired woman. I can tell. I watched them together while you were asleep. They really care a lot about each other."

Isabelle steeled herself against his words. She didn't like to hear them. She didn't want the jealousy that immediately came to her mind. Jeremiah was in love with her, not Victoriana. She knew it was a fact.

Still, there was always a nagging doubt when it came to their relationship, and being the kind of creeping insect Percy was, he'd picked up on it.

Isabelle wondered how long he'd been in Low Branch.

The last thing she wanted was to hold a casual conversation with the man. She couldn't imagine saying, "So, how long have you been in town?"

She was holding her arm tight to her, despite the fact his hand was still wrapped around her wrist.

"I don't believe a word that comes out of your despicable mouth, Percy Andrews. You need to go back to Berkenshire and let me live my life."

He shook his head. "Can't," he replied simply.

"What are you talking about?" she asked. "All you need to do is get on the train and go. It's that easy. That's all you have to do."

She tried again to pull her hand away, but he was

still holding her too tightly. She was beginning to lose all the blood in her hand.

"You're hurting me," she hissed, glaring him in the eye. "You don't have the right to come and take me away from here. This is my home now, and I'm going to marry Jeremiah next week."

She hated the look of smug revulsion on Percy's face.

"You won't be marrying him next week, Isabelle. You might as well get that through your head."

Isabelle reminded herself he had no power over her. She straightened her spine to the best of her ability in her weakened state.

"You can't... you can't do anything to stop it," she said, hating that she'd hesitated and had to start again. It made her seem insecure.

She was frightened of him but still confident. She thought about the gun inside. Maybe she should talk him into coming in. She could get it and take a shot in the sky as Jeremiah suggested. That would get Brock's attention. And Victoriana's. And even Clarice's.

Doubt slid through her when she thought about the women in the big ranch house. Was Victoriana really her friend? Maybe she had conspired with Clarice and gotten Isabelle to reveal things about

Berkenshire she might not have told someone she didn't consider a friend. That would certainly count out Mrs. Clarice Connelly.

Maybe the only way they'd been able to find Percy was because Isabelle felt comfortable talking to the woman about her past in Berkenshire and how she and Jeremiah had met.

"Who are you working with?" she asked, narrowing her eyes and pulling on her arm. "Let me go. I don't owe you anything. I'm not yours to come and take back to Virginia."

"My father said we are to be wed by the end of the month. He said that when I found you, I was to inform you of that."

Isabelle snorted. "What in heaven's name are you talking about? He isn't my father. He can't tell me what to do, and neither can you."

Percy looked angry. "I thought you respected my father."

"I do. And I also don't believe he would send you here with a message like that."

Percy's face darkened.

"Are you calling me a liar?"

Isabelle stiffened, casting angry eyes at him. "Yes."

Percy's right arm came around and flew through

the air toward her. She moved her eyes up just in time to see the heavy backside of a pistol as it came toward her head.

It made impact right above her left eye, and everything went black.

25

———

The sound of raised voices met Jeremiah's ears before he'd reached the outer path to go to his ranch house. He pushed his heels into the horse's backside to get it moving faster, and the animal broke into a run.

He rounded the last curve before he could see the house and peered closely at the front porch squinting.

It was Victoriana and his mother.

Terrified to know what had happened, he got to the porch as quick as his horse could get him and jumped from the saddle. He landed roughly in the dirt, sending clouds up around his ankles. He took the steps two at a time, unable to believe the two fighting women hadn't detected his presence yet.

"You've done something," Victoriana was shrieking, pacing back and forth, her eyes on the ground, her face red. "You've done something with her, or you've had that man from Virginia come and get her. It had to be you. I know it was you. I saw you in the bungalow that day. When she was gone. You were looking through her personal things, weren't you? I should have told her. I should have told her."

"None of this is your business," the older woman yelled back, her voice tougher than Jeremiah had ever heard it before. "This is going to work out to your benefit. You will be the one wed to my son. You will be the one running this ranch and enjoying a wealthy life. Let her be with that mayor's son. That's the life she should be leading. You are too good for something simple."

"It's not your right to tell me what I'm good or not good for."

It was at this point that Jeremiah landed on the top step of the porch and reached out to push his arms between them. He broke them apart as Victoriana came stomping over to his mother, one finger jabbing the air accusingly.

"All right, all right, that's enough of that," he announced, pushing through his fear that something had happened to Isabelle to speak with an authoritative, strong tone. "What's going on?"

"She let him take her," Victoriana instantly cried out. Those were the words he didn't want to hear. Probably the only words in the world that could easily break his heart.

"What... do you mean?" He moved his eyes to his mother. "What's she talking about?" he asked, his voice dropping a few temperature levels.

Clarice shook her head, sighing heavily. She lifted her nose in an arrogant way that Jeremiah found abhorrent. He would make sure none of his children ended up self-centered this way. "I was doing what was best for my son," she insisted, "and the woman he should be marrying deserves a happy, fulfilled life."

"Again, you can't tell me that," Victoriana said with more venom in her voice than Jeremiah expected. He stepped back, letting the woman speak. He wanted to get to the bottom of this and find out where Isabelle was taken and how long ago. But first, he had to let these women get out their grievances, or nothing would be accomplished but a lot of unproductive arguing.

"That's enough," he roared. He took his mother by her shoulders and forced her to look at him.

"Did you bring that man over here, Mother?"

She didn't answer. In fact, the expression on her face remained arrogant and cold. That was all he needed to know his answer.

He pushed her back gently, letting go in a way that would keep her from stumbling or losing her balance.

"So, it was you. Where is she, Mother? Where did he take her?"

"I'm not going to tell you."

Jeremiah couldn't believe his mother's audacity. Nor her childishness.

"I can't believe you are doing this to me," he growled, struggling to hold onto his temper. He pictured in his mind the many places Percy could have taken Isabelle, including on the way back to Virginia. He took a step closer to his mother, despite having pushed her away. He set his eyes on her and growled, "I hope you understand I will go to the ends of the earth to find that woman. I love her. I'm not letting her go. Not you or anyone else will keep me from marrying her."

The smug look on his mother's face made him feel a little sick to his stomach.

"You will have to marry Victoriana next week if you can't find her by then or give up the fortune to your uncle. Is that what you want? Are you going to give up everything?"

"You have got to stop putting me in your schemes, old woman," Victoriana snarled. She looked at Jeremiah and followed up with, "If you want to save your fortune, I'll marry you so you can get it. But we will have it annulled, and I don't care about any blow to any reputation I might have. I'm not going to stand between you and your ranch, and I will help you find her."

Jeremiah nodded at the woman. "Thank you, Vicky. But I don't think that's gonna be necessary. My mother is going to tell us where Percy has taken Isabelle. Aren't you, mother?"

"Exactly why would I do that?" Clarice asked, her snide look making her face very ugly.

"Because if you don't and I decide to give up my fortune and not marry Vicky, you'll be out of a home and property and everything you own except what Uncle Daniel gives you. Won't you love living on an allowance like a small child, Mother? Always at the mercy of my uncle? Your deceased husband's brother? Who has a family and a wife of his own? Think about that and tell me what you want to do. Because I don't think you want to be under Uncle Daniel's thumb."

He could see he'd made an impact on his mother. Her breath had quickened. He could see her chest rising and falling as she stared at him, unblinking.

Finally, she moved away from him, looking off into the distance over the field. Jeremiah wondered if she was trying to give him a sign of some kind. He took a step toward her, but she held up her hand.

"Give me a minute, if you don't mind."

Anger lit up Jeremiah's nerves. "You don't need a minute, Mother. You need to tell me where they've gone. Tell me. I have to know. I have to get her back."

"You won't turn down a fortune. Vicky has already offered—"

"Mother." Jeremiah was a few seconds away from throttling his mother. It was taking everything he had to keep his temper. He couldn't lose control. He had to be the man of the family. Besides, it was beginning hurt more than anger him. How could she treat him like a child?

On the one hand, when his mother jumped at his barking voice, it made him feel a certain amount of satisfaction. But she still had not told him what he wanted to know. And until she did, he would bark and growl at her like a dog.

He took another step closer, glaring at her back.

"Tell me. Tell me where she is. Tell me, or I will never speak to you again. I will marry Vicky. I will keep my fortune. And I will banish you from the property and all your worldly goods. You will keep the clothes on your back and a nicely packed trunk."

As he spoke, she slowly turned around, her eyes wide with fear. His voice was like ice, exactly the way he wanted it. She looked terrified.

"There's no need to go that far," she said frantically. "I just wanted what's best for you, that's all. Not—"

"It's not for you to decide," he roared. "Tell me where she is."

After another moment of frozen hesitation, his mother said, "He's taking her to the train station. Keeping her out of sight until the four-fifteen."

Jeremiah's eyes darted to Victoriana, who lifted her arm and looked at her watch.

"We have fifteen minutes, Jeremiah," she said.

All Jeremiah could think about on the way to the train station was that he'd been late when he picked Isabelle up. She'd insisted the train was early, but he'd discovered his watch was, in fact, five minutes behind, and he'd had to adjust it. He'd never told her he'd realized the mistake was his, and she'd never brought it up again.

It was Victoriana's watch that had given them the time, and he hoped hers was accurate. He'd pulled her up on the back of his horse since the animal was saddled up and ready to go. They'd traveled a long way, but he'd taken it at a good pace so as not to wear the horse down.

He heard the horn of the train blaring, heard the sounds of the engines and the hiss of the steam.

"Hurry, hurry, hurry," Victoriana called out frantically behind him.

"We'll make it," he cried, encouraging himself as well as her. "We'll make it. We'll make it."

"We have to," she responded.

They were in the dirt parking lot with one minute to spare, according to Victoriana's watch, but the time didn't matter as much as the position of the train. It was still motionless next to the platform where a good number of people were milling about as if they had nothing better to do with their lives.

Jeremiah was annoyed with them all. They were in his way. He was looking for the woman he loved, who could be hidden anywhere on the train or in the station.

Or somewhere nearby.

He swept his eyes over his surroundings as they passed, wondering if she was hidden in the trees and bushes. A shack or a shed behind those tall trees, in the midst of the woods. Where was she?

His heart raced as fast as his horse getting to the station. He pulled the animal to a halt, and Victoriana immediately slid off the back. She was already heading toward the three steps leading up to the platform by the train.

Jeremiah wasn't far behind her. He took his cue

from her and began looking in the windows of the train first. Isabelle wasn't anywhere on the platform. He leaned over to glance inside the small building where tickets were bought, and luggage was received.

When he turned from that window, he caught sight of Victoriana near the end of the train to his right. He went to the open doorway and went up, holding onto the railing as he leaned in and back, looking through windows at the people in the car to his right.

She wasn't in there. Not that he could see.

He thought back to what his mother had said. Percy was keeping her hidden. To Jeremiah, that meant she could be disguised. He could have made her unconscious somehow, drugged her, or gotten her drunk so she would pass out.

Jeremiah didn't want to believe Percy would hurt Isabelle to knock her out.

He pushed further onto the landing and passed through the small door to enter the car to his left. He scanned the people in the car. They all had their heads down. The only two who weren't looking at books or newspapers or ledgers were a man and woman who seemed to be having an intimate, serious conversation.

The woman was facing him and had dark brown hair. She was taller and heavier than Isabelle. There was no chance she was his lost love.

He wished he'd had a chance to see Percy with his own eyes. If he knew ahead of time exactly what the man looked like, he would have an easier time spotting him. He might appear to be traveling alone when he actually had her hidden away somewhere.

Jeremiah's heart trembled at the bad thoughts he was having. What had Percy done to Isabelle?

His ears sharpened to the sounds around him when he thought he heard his name being called.

"Jeremiah." It came again, and he recognized Victoriana's voice. He shot to the door he'd come in and jumped down the stairs, turning to find the woman in the small crowd.

"Vicky,"

The woman emerged from behind a couple and hurried over to him.

"I didn't find her," she said. "And I don't even know if she's on the train. She might not be. Maybe she's nearby, and he's waiting for—"

At that moment, the train horn blasted through the air, and Victoriana covered her ears, wincing. When it stopped, she said, "Waiting for the last call to board. But that would be now. He's got to come now."

"We have to get on the train," Jeremiah stated. "We can't stay here."

"But what if they aren't on the train?" Victoriana cried out in despair. "What if he decided to take her on a stagecoach instead? He can't be trusted. What he told your mother might not be what he really planned to do. And what if they are hidden somewhere around here and she's hurt and he can't get her on the train?"

Jeremiah shook his head, grabbing her arm. "We have to get on the train. I have to trust my instincts, and I think she's on there."

"But we don't have tickets." He couldn't believe that's what she was worried about at that point.

"I'll buy them if the attendant comes around before we find Isabelle. I know he's on the train. He's the kind of man that will get away from here as fast as he can. He won't linger. And he won't be clever enough to take the stagecoach instead of the train."

There was absolutely no way for Jeremiah to know such information. He was aware of that fact. Still, as he'd told Victoriana, he had to trust his instincts. They'd never let him down before.

"Well, come on then, let's go." Victoriana

grabbed Jeremiah's arm and pushed him aggressively toward the train. He was momentarily amused but managed to get up on the train and turn to give her a hand, as well.

They went through the car to their left, the one Jeremiah had just left. They went to the next one and passed through the middle aisle. There were three more passenger cars and then nothing but coal and other earthly elements being transported by train, along with the luggage car before the caboose.

The car after the one they entered first was empty. The one after that had three people in it, and none of them resembled Isabelle or her description of Percy. Additionally, they didn't look up when Jeremiah entered, and he was sure Percy would look.

They came up to the door to the last car, and Jeremiah pushed it open for Victoriana. She went through first.

Jeremiah moved to come up behind her and close the door to the train. They could hear and feel it rolling into motion. They would soon be well on their way eastward, heading toward Virginia, which was probably one of its last stops. Not that Jeremiah would know about the route. He'd never gone to the east in his travels.

He'd only taken one step when he nearly ran

into Victoriana, who had suddenly stopped. He looked over her head and saw why immediately.

In the middle of the car on the left side, there was a woman lying with a blanket over her and a man sitting opposite her. The man's back was to them.

Jeremiah's heart slammed in his chest. Anger rose up, and he struggled to hold it in.

The man who could only be Percy turned and looked at them. His eyes widened, as did his mouth. He looked terrified, and all the blood drained from his face.

This reaction didn't last for very long. In the next moment, he had jumped to the other side where the woman, Isabelle, was lying on her side, yanking her into a sitting position. Her head flopped forward. She wasn't conscious.

Seeing her in that state made Jeremiah's control over his temper dissolve.

He pushed Victoriana out of the way and leaped toward Percy.

27

He thought he was about to land a punch. He didn't expect Percy to grab Isabelle's shoulders and shove her in between the two of them.

He pulled back just in time but lost his balance in the process. He heard Victoriana call out his name. After going tumbling, Jeremiah bound back to his feet and turned around swiftly. He saw Victoriana trying to grab at Isabelle's arms, calling her name, too.

"Wake up, Isabelle. Wake up. Wake up. Come back with us."

Isabelle stirred, which was a relief to Jeremiah. Percy was facing him, pressed back against the booth, still holding the woman in front of him. Jeremiah wondered what he expected to accomplish by that. All he was doing was prolonging the inevitable. If Isabelle never woke up and remained unconscious the whole time, Percy wouldn't be able to move from that spot without getting arrested or taken down somehow.

And when she did come back to life, Percy was going to be in real trouble. Jeremiah had no doubt she was going to be extremely angry, and he wasn't quite sure what a woman of her Irish descent might do when pushed that far.

"Vicky, go get an attendant," he barked at the woman, keeping his eyes on Percy. Every few seconds, he dropped his eyes to Isabelle. "I've got this."

He didn't like the look of Percy Andrews, the mayor's son. He looked arrogant, with a long nose he probably kept pointed up in the air just like his mother, Clarice. They would be a good pair. He imagined they'd gotten along quite well in their correspondence with each other. He was wiry and had a natural sneer that made Jeremiah want to punch him.

"What do you think you're doing?" Jeremiah asked in a low, steady voice. Maybe he could reason with the man. It was certainly better than shooting each other. But if that was what Percy insisted on, that's what would happen. "You aren't going to get her back to Virginia. Even if you do, don't you see she will run from you the first chance she gets? And she will come back to me. When that happens, I can guarantee you'll never see her again. I doubt you will see the light of freedom again."

He hesitated, hoping he wasn't pushing too far.

"You're already in so far, Percy. Why don't you stop this now before it goes *too* far."

"Don't call me Percy," the man growled. "You don't know me. You aren't my friend."

"Well, buddy, I'm afraid I ain't callin' you Mr. Andrews. That's reserved for someone I respect, and that ain't you."

Percy sneered. He lifted one hand and slid it comfortably underneath Isabelle's chin, wrapping his fingers around her neck.

Jeremiah's heart almost seized and stopped. He lifted one hand in the air.

"Don't hurt her, buddy," he snapped. "That's not gonna do a thing. She ain't done a thing to you. She hasn't done a thing, you hear me? She doesn't deserve to die for being in love with someone that isn't you."

"She didn't leave to come to Texas because she

loved you," Percy growled in a snide voice. "She left because she was tired of Berkenshire. She doesn't love you now. She told me so."

Jeremiah wasn't fazed. He knew the truth. He shook his head at the man.

"I'm not falling for your lies, bud. Let her go. Don't hurt her. You hurt her, and you're gonna get hurt. We aren't gonna let you off this train."

Anger was making it difficult for Jeremiah to think straight. Percy was lucky he had enough of his wits together not to just blast the man away.

Percy just smiled. Isabelle's eyes opened wide. She looked at Jeremiah first before a panicked look came across her face.

"Jer—"

Percy's demeanor changed once again. He seemed to get angry that she had woken up even though he'd been jerking her around like a rag doll. What did he expect?

He pressed against her neck with his hand. The only reason Jeremiah knew he was applying pressure was that Isabelle's hands flew up to her neck, and she pried at Percy's hand, scratching him with her nails.

He growled at her and shook her by her neck, making her gag.

Jeremiah had had enough of that. He pounced on them both, using both hands to snatch Isabelle out of Percy's grip while the man didn't expect it and tossed her to the bench behind him to the left.

In the next moment, he and Percy were grappling, rolling around on the floor of the train, bumping with every move on the tracks, both roaring in anger. There was no way Jeremiah would let this man take the woman he loved away from him. Not to another state and most definitely not to Heaven.

Jeremiah managed to roll over and over until Percy was below him. He got in several punches before the wiry man was able to maneuver himself around and flip Jeremiah over.

As soon as the man was above him, Jeremiah raised both hands and put them around Percy's neck, squeezing the way he'd done to Isabelle.

He never got the chance to find out if he was actually capable of choking Percy out because a second later, someone came up above them and whacked Percy on the head with something that made a loud clang off his skull.

His eyes opened wide, and he fell to the side. Seeing this was about to happen, Jeremiah raised both arms to block the man's fall on top of him. He caught Percy and shoved him to the side, making him fall off.

Breathing heavy, Jeremiah got to his feet and lowered himself to rest with his hands on his knees.

He hung his head for a moment. A soft hand on his back told him Isabelle had come over to him.

"What... what was that... who was that... Did you..."

"It wasn't me," Isabelle whispered, leaning down to his ear. Her breath on his skin made him tingle all over. "The attendant came back with Vicky and hit him over the head with a baton. He's going to arrest him or at least hold him until the sheriff at the next stop can take him."

Jeremiah pulled in a deep breath, sighing in relief.

"Thank God," he said, shaking his head.

"I'm thanking you," Isabelle responded, her eyes soft on his. He felt a tug on his heart. "You saved me. You didn't have to come after me. You could have decided I wanted to go with Percy and never come after me."

Jeremiah shook his head. "I couldn't do that. I believed you when you said you loved me."

Isabelle blinked at him. "But," she replied in a soft voice, "I never said I loved you."

He chuckled softly, running two fingers under her chin. "Not with words you didn't. Not yet. It was your eyes. Your touch. Your kiss. And your laugh, too, when I tell you a joke that really isn't funny."

She giggled, a sound that grabbed his heart.

"That's how you decided you could trust me?"

Jeremiah nodded. "I trust my heart. I trust my instincts. And I trust you."

"That's so sweet of you to say, Jeremiah." She touched his cheeks with her fingers, gazing into his eyes lovingly. "Since you feel that way, I guess I don't even need to say it, do I?"

Jeremiah blinked at her, grabbing her around the waist and pulling her to him.

"I think I want to hear it if you don't mind."

"You do?"

He knew she was teasing him.

He nodded. "I do."

"All right." She lifted up on her tiptoes and pressed her lips against his. When she pulled back, she left her eyes on his. "I love you, Jeremiah."

He smiled. "I love you, too, Isabelle."

28

Isabelle felt the train coming to a stop. Jeremiah had taken her to a different car to wait with Victoriana for the next town on the train schedule.

Her head was hurting, and her neck felt tight as if Percy's hand was still around it. Even when he'd been holding her that way, she'd still be sure Jeremiah would stop the situation before she died. She was confident Jeremiah would always protect her. Especially now, after seeing the lengths he would go to for her to be safe.

It touched her, too, that Victoriana had come along. That was a sign of a true friend. She would be sad to see the woman go. She wondered if speaking would make her throat hurt after being squeezed the way it was. She cleared it, her eyes on Victoriana. Her friend lifted her eyebrows curiously.

"Yes?" she said, amused.

"When are you planning to leave us?" Isabelle asked, hoping the words she used and the tone of her voice would clue her friend in that she didn't really want her to leave at all.

Victoriana's face fell. Jeremiah's eyes darted to Isabelle and then to Victoriana.

"I've been wondering the same thing," he said. "I think you should know by now that we would miss you very much if you just up and left. Surely you could stay in Low Branch. I'm sure there's really nothing to make you go back to the town you came from. Right?"

Isabelle heard his teasing tone and realized he'd been thinking the same thing as her. He didn't want her to go. She turned a direct look at Victoriana, demanding an answer with her eyes.

"You don't want me to go?" she asked. "Don't you think that would be one too many women in the house? I think a lot of people would be very confused by that."

"There's going to be a little bungalow by a creek available after next week," Isabelle mentioned slyly.

Victoriana pressed her lips together, smiling

through the expression. "You really want me to take your bungalow from you? I know you'll be in the main house, but I had figured you'd want to at least go there when Jeremiah here starts getting under your skin and you need some time to yourself."

"Hey," Jeremiah pretended to be offended and hurt.

Victoriana laughed softly and was quickly joined by both Isabelle and Jeremiah.

"You know I don't mean any offense, Jeremiah. If the two of you want me to stay here in Low Branch, I don't see why I can't. I'll have to find something to do with myself, though. You two aren't going to want me around in the way. Especially not for the first month or twelve. You'll be too in love with each other."

Isabelle's face flushed. It might be the truth, but it was something she'd never felt before and was still so nervous about.

THE THREE GOT off the train in Spruceville, a town with so many spruce trees Isabelle had no trouble figuring out the source of the name. They dined in a small restaurant on the corner of the train station building and marveled at the genius of putting the restaurant there. Jeremiah presumed the owners were making money hand over fist.

Isabelle had no interest in knowing what happened to Percy. She left the procedures up to Jeremiah, who had spent the majority of the time when they first stepped off the train in Spruceville explaining exactly what had happened with the man. He told her she would need to provide details and that they would come back in the next few days to give statements to the judge whenever he visited next. Until then, Percy would be held in the jailhouse.

Jeremiah told her he would be able to contact his father. For a moment, Isabelle wondered what Barney Andrews would do.

And then she forgot all about it.

THAT EVENING, Jeremiah set about making a fire in the fireplace for her in the bungalow. She was comfortable there, especially because Clarice was still in the main house. Jeremiah would have to deal with that for her, too. She wasn't a confrontational person. She wanted everyone to like her. Why

Clarice would dislike her the way she did was hurtful. She didn't even want to think about it.

She put her feet up on the couch, stretching out on her side.

Jeremiah came over to the couch and stayed on the floor, sitting on the rug, his back against the couch she was lying on. He was staring into the fire. She was amazed at how handsome he looked, his profile lit up with flames dancing with shadows over his tan skin.

She ran one hand through his brown hair instinctively, causing him to smile self-consciously. He lowered his eyes and chin at the same time. She ran her hand down the back of his head, leaving it resting against his neck. She would never tire of the tingles she felt when he touched her. She hoped that sensation lasted her entire lifetime.

He turned his head to catch her gaze. She lost her breath, overwhelmed by the love she saw in his eyes. She wished she could capture that moment in time and keep it in a bottle forever. But it would have to reside in her memory. And there it would stay, that one moment, the look in his eyes, her hand upon his neck.

"Please tell me there aren't any other men pursuing your hand with such intensity that we might have to go through this again. I know you are desirable, but I don't know how many times I can do this."

Isabelle giggled. "What if there was? What if I had a hundred suitors trying to capture my hand, and it will take only the kiss of true love to save me from them one by one?"

Jeremiah's eyebrows shot up. "A hundred kisses from your true love? I think I can handle the kisses, my darling. It's the fist-fighting, heart-pounding terror that you're going to be killed and the thought of possibly dying myself that I can't do a hundred times. I'll be old before my time."

Isabelle had to laugh. She loved his sense of humor. She patted the back of his neck.

"Rest assured, there is no one else coming after me. That man was the only one who wanted me in Berkenshire, and I must be honest, there weren't any at all that interested me, so it was all right that I wasn't welcomed, I suppose you could say. I can't believe even he came after me."

"He put bruises on your arms, grabbing you," Jeremiah said solemnly, losing his smile. "He was a dangerous man. It's good that we were able to stop him. If it hadn't been you, it might have been another woman who didn't have anyone to save her. Now Percy won't be able to hurt any women at all."

"If his father doesn't get him off with a warning."

Isabelle hoped that wouldn't happen. A bit of nervous anxiety slid through her but dissipated when Jeremiah said, "I've asked the sheriff in Spruceville to let us know what happens. If he's let go, we'll be on our guard and watching out for him. You'll be in the main house with me, so I'll be able to keep you safe."

"We will need more locks on the bungalow if Victoriana stays there," Isabelle mentioned. "If he thinks she's me, she might be in danger. I won't let anything bad happen to her."

Jeremiah shook his head. "No, my darling. We won't let anything happen to her. I'm glad we are all friends. She's a nice woman."

"She is. I bet if we tried, we could find a good man for her."

Jeremiah grinned, lifting one hand to rest it on her arm over his shoulder. "Let's just concentrate on each other for a while, all right?"

Isabelle giggled, nodding. "All right."

29

When Isabelle woke up the next morning, she jerked awake and sat up immediately, fear making her heart pound. She looked down and saw Jeremiah was no longer in front of the couch.

Soft sounds behind her made Isabelle lift up and look over the back of the couch toward the kitchen. It was open to the front room so she could see him at the stove, hovering over a pot. The scent of coffee met her nose.

"That smells wonderful," she said softly.

He turned around and gazed at her warmly. "Do you feel all right?" he asked.

She nodded, pushing her hands through her

hair. "I do. I feel free. I didn't even know I wasn't free before. Now I really feel it."

He chuckled, picking up the pot and pouring the coffee into a cup. He held it up.

"Do you want sugar?"

"Two please and a dash of milk from the icebox."

A few moments later, Jeremiah was handing her the cup before he dropped to the couch next to her. She pulled her legs up and blew on the steaming liquid in the cup.

"This is nice," she murmured, grinning at him.

"It is. And just think. In eight days, you will wake up in the main house with me. You won't have to wait for your coffee. Cook gets up well early enough to make it. But we can cook ourselves whenever we want. If you want to make me a dinner, I wouldn't mind."

She liked the sound of that, nodding. "I'm going to do that for you. I hope that you will return the favor, though. The meals you've made me so far have been excellent. Delicious."

"If I had time, I would make dinner for you every night."

He held out his hand, and she rested hers in his. He leaned toward her, placing a soft kiss on her cheek.

"Isabelle, I want to ask you something."

She gazed at him, sure in her heart it was going to be something good. She nodded, giving him the softest, warmest smile she could.

"Will you marry me?"

She was taken off guard by the question. She'd thought that was already a given. But then she realized what he was doing. He'd never asked her. Not formally. It had been a mutual agreement, almost like a business deal up until now.

Now he was asking because he loved her. Because he wanted to be her husband.

"I want to spend the rest of my life with you, Isabelle. Not just because you came here to marry me so I could retain my fortune. I want you to know that's not why I'm marrying you. That was how it started. I will admit that. But you knew that already. I want you to know I mean this from my heart. I want to marry you. Will you be my wife?"

Isabelle listened to his words with a heart growing in size with every word. Tears came to her eyes. Her hands moved to her face, covering first her cheeks, then her mouth. She nodded and knew she would have to say the words out loud, or it just wouldn't be right.

"I love you, Jeremiah Connelly," she managed to

get out through her tears. "I want to marry you. Yes, I will. I will be your wife. I will love you for the rest of my life."

He stood up, putting his hand down to help her up. She took it, and he lifted her to feet, hearing a strange sound outside.

Turning to the window, Isabelle was sure she saw a shadow pass by. She heard the strangest sound out there and moved directly to the window to look out.

Jeremiah was laughing behind her, holding her hand until they were too far away to continue touching. He stayed where he was, crossing his arms over his chest, a satisfied look on his handsome face.

"What is going on out there?" she asked curiously.

"Come on out with me and see for yourself," Jeremiah replied.

Isabelle went to the door, looking up at him with apprehensive eyes. There were people out on the lawn. Lots of people.

Jeremiah opened the door and held it open so she could go through it first.

Isabelle was amazed by what she saw. It seemed the people had been there for at least an hour. She turned from the left to right, watching children running around dropping rose petals on the ground. A tall arch was being constructed quickly with iron parts that seemed to fit perfectly together.

What amazed her the most was the number of flowers. The variety of types and colors was astounding. How could anyone pull this together so quickly? He must have been planning it for a while.

"After everything we've been through," Jeremiah said from behind her, making her turn and gaze lovingly at him, "I didn't want to wait another day to marry you. You said yes last night. The flower shop will have to close down until a new shipment comes in because I bought them all."

Isabelle couldn't help laughing with delight. "I was wondering where they all came from."

"There won't be anything necessarily special about what you see here," Jeremiah said. "It's only special because I went to town early and rounded everyone and everything up so that we could get married today. Folks are taking the day off work or their regular schedule, Isabelle. Just for you."

Isabelle's heart melted as she took in the friendly faces around her, dolling the place up to make it pretty for her special day.

Jeremiah came up behind her and put his arm

around her waist. She turned her head to look up at him. Her heart was so full that she thought it might burst.

"This is absolutely amazing, Jeremiah. I never expected you to do something like this."

Brock came out of nowhere and was suddenly in front of them. He blocked the rising sun from Isabelle's face, and the rays shone around him like an aura. Isabelle smiled at him.

"I hope you have a good day today, Isabelle. I'm glad you and Jeremiah are doing this. He needed a good woman in his life."

"You never told me that," Jeremiah said in a teasing voice. "Not even once."

Brock chuckled. "A man is allowed to keep some thoughts to himself, boss. Especially when they're about the boss." He flicked one index finger between himself and Jeremiah.

They both laughed.

"Congratulations, Isabelle. Jeremiah. I'm glad to be working for you both."

"We're glad to have you around, Brock," Jeremiah responded in a friendly voice. "Don't you forget you're bringin' up the rings for us."

Isabelle raised her eyebrows at Jeremiah, turning her head to him again and leaning to the side slightly. She hadn't known he'd gotten special rings for them already.

He laughed when he saw the look on her face. "Yes, I bought them. A few days ago. I've had them in my room all this time."

"So you think of everything," she teased, "just in case we did this early?"

He nodded. "That's right."

"You were that confident I would say yes?"

Jeremiah lifted his eyebrows. "Was there a reason not to be confident?"

She snuggled up against him, giggling. "No," she responded. "No reason at all."

"I've got some work to do to finish this up," Brock said quickly. "I'll see you two at the altar."

"Oh, Jeremiah," Isabelle sighed as Brock hopped down the few steps to the grass and strolled away. "You really outdid yourself. How will anyone else ever throw a wedding here in Low Branch again? No one can outdo this."

Jeremiah pressed his face into her neck, kissing her gently.

"If they're smart," he said in a quiet voice, "they will figure out their own way of expressing their deep love for the woman they are about to marry."

Isabelle sighed, closing her eyes and leaning

back against him. She knew for a fact at that very moment that she would never have to worry about her safety or happiness ever again.

She had Jeremiah. He was all she needed.

EPILOGUE

Jeremiah looked out over the pasture at the cattle grazing in the distance.

He was remembering that day a year ago when he'd married his sweet Isabelle after that harrowing experience on the train.

She was supposed to meet him on the trail to go for a ride with him. It was their favorite pastime. No one knew, but when they went for their rides all over the Connelly land, they sang together, sometimes loud, sometimes soft, sometimes completely off-key, just to be funny. Isabelle wasn't as good as he was at making up lyrics off the top of his head. He could use their surroundings and make his song sound elegant.

He had something planned for her today for their

first anniversary. She had told him the one thing she really wanted to do on their anniversary, other than the party with their friends, was to go on a ride.

When he saw her in the distance, he was a little surprised to see she was not wearing her usual dress. She was, in fact, in riding gear. As she got closer, he realized something was different about her. He tilted his head to the side, trying to figure out what it was before she got there. Surely she was going to tell him what was different. Did she have a new haircut? Was it just that she was wearing trousers and he rarely saw her in that type of gear?

It was something else, something significant.

He was ashamed he didn't know what it was.

"Hello, my darling," he said when she approached, leaning to give her a kiss. She pulled her horse up alongside his and returned the kiss.

"Hello, dear."

"Happy anniversary," he said. She laughed. It was only the fourth time he'd told her that since they got up in the morning.

"Happy anniversary to you, too."

"All right, now tell me. There's something different about you. I can't put my finger on it. Please tell me before I lose my mind."

She laughed softly, giving him the sweetest look he'd ever seen.

"Oh, you. You know me too well."

"You don't usually wear this riding gear," he said, dropping his eyes to sweep them over her body. "I reckon there has to be somethin' going on that I'm missing."

She pursed her lips. "Well, I have gained some weight."

"You've gained weight." He repeated the words back to her while running his eyes over her body. She was right. That was what had made the difference in his eyes.

"Well, you are looking very healthy. I love you, skinny or fat."

When she laughed again, it was in a different voice. A voice that made him blink at her. What was she thinking? Why was she acting so strange?

It suddenly dawned on him why a woman might gain weight after getting married.

"Isabelle..." he said, drawing his horse to a stop. They had only been meandering slowly down the path anyway. Neither were really looking where they were going, so the horses were making their own way.

"Yes?" she asked him slyly, a mischievous look on her face.

"Are you... are we going to have a baby?"

The biggest grin grew on Isabelle's face, giving him his answer. His heart leaped into his throat.

"You... we... we're going to have a child. My first child. Our first. My firstborn son."

"Hey now," Isabelle laughed. "You don't know that it will be a boy. It might be a girl."

"And if it is, may God bless her to look like you and not me." Jeremiah was overjoyed. He wanted to shout from the hilltops. He was going to be a father. He couldn't wait to see what the baby looked like. That was the first thing that came to his mind.

"I kind of hope that, too," Isabelle replied, still laughing.

"Well, well," he said, feeling satisfied. "I think this day is going to turn out to be mighty fine. So many people we have to tell. We'll have to make a lot of plans. Build one of the rooms into a nursery. Right near our room, of course, one of those. I hope you don't want a nanny. I'd like for us to raise our children together. The two of us."

"Yes, yes," Isabelle replied, nodding. "I want to raise my children. I don't need any help doing it."

"Are you sure you should be riding?" Worry for

her filled his chest, making him feel apprehensive. He felt like ordering her to go back to the house and sit down and stay there for the next seven or eight months, however far along she was.

She just laughed at his question. "Yes, I can be riding. I can ride all the way until the end. My body will protect my child. Don't worry about that."

"That's good. That's good. Do you need anything? What do you want me to do?"

Her answer made his heart sing. He felt blessed beyond comprehension, having the woman of his dreams on his arm, having his first child... there couldn't be anything more fulfilling. His life had changed so much in the last year that he barely recognized it anymore.

"All I want you to do," she said, taking his hand in one hand and holding onto the saddle horn with the other, "is love me no matter how upset I get. I will be grumpy and will be in bad moods some-times. I will be angry for no reason. That's what the ladies are telling me. As you might know, I've never been through this before. But if you can just get through this first one with me, just holding my hand and reminding me how much you love me, I think we'll be just fine. Then with any more chil-dren we have, we'll just keep getting better at it. I just want to get through this with you. Just be with me."

"I'll never leave your side," he replied, "unless you ask me to. I won't be over you all the time, but yes, I'll be by your side every step of the way. I promise. I swear it. I'm yours, my love. I love you."

"I love you, Jeremiah. You're going to be such a wonderful father."

Click here for more Blythe Carver books!

Sign up for the newsletter to be notified of new releases.

Click on link for
Newsletter
or put this in your browser window:

landing.mailerlite.com/webforms/landing/p6l2s1